CW00919299

THE GOOD CHILD

CHARLOTTE BARNES

BLOODHOUND
BOOKS

First published in 2023 by Bloodhound Books.

www.bloodhoundbooks.com

Print ISBN: 978-1-5040-8693-6

Mum, thank you for always putting up with the strange, hypothetical questions – and for always being my Annie xx

PROLOGUE

I didn't want him to be cold, so I tucked his jacket in around him. It was his favourite; one that I'd bought him for Christmas – or his birthday, I forget. I hadn't noticed when I saw him earlier in the night, that that's what he was wearing. It was such a happy memory, though, when I did realise, because he'd wanted the jacket for ages. It was stupidly expensive, and I hadn't even liked it that much when he pointed it out, two months before – so it must have been Christmas when I bought it, because I remember saving money through October and part of November to make sure I could get it. And – and I hadn't even liked it. Still, I tucked it in around him, because I didn't want him to be cold. But more than anything, I just didn't want him to be dead.

PART 1

ANNIE

CHAPTER ONE

It was one of those perfectly cold mornings. The heating had clicked on sometime during the night and the house hummed with the tick-tick-whir of it. From the kitchen window I could see the beginnings of the garden; the ground was frosted over with a wintertime glitter and there was a horror film mist that lingered over the rest of the landscape still. I couldn't see right down to the end of the lawn yet, and I longed for those slow moments when the chilled duvet would peel back and make way for the day. Burnt offerings popped up from the toaster then, and pulled me out of the moment. But at least my coffee had brewed right; two heaped spoons and one sweetener, no milk – and I thought of Theo as I took the first sips. 'As black as your soul that is,' he used to say, and I smiled at the memory. I threw two seeded slices of ashen bread into the bin and gave up on the idea of breakfast. Instead, I went back to the coffee and the garden and the quiet lull of 'Mr Sandman'; a jazz cover that my streaming service had recommended. I was in the middle of asking Mr Sandman to bring me a dream when–

Thud. Thud-thud-thud.

'Need a lift?'

Jessica skidded into the room in time to hear the question. 'Shit, I'm so late, Mum.'

I sighed and smiled at once. 'Come on, grab a breakfast bar and I'll drive you in.' I set my drink down with some resentment; how often does the perfect morning cup of coffee come around? I stole one last look at the garden then turned to catch my daughter slathering marmalade onto a slice of bread. 'You're an animal.'

'Raised by wolves, me,' she said around a mouthful.

'Get your bag, you feral thing.' I grabbed a breakfast bar from the cupboard on my way through the room. 'And take this, you might want elevenses.'

'Mum…'

'Jess, it's a bloody breakfast bar. I'm not sending you in with a full English.'

'Fine, whatever.' She snatched the bar and wedged it into the front pocket of her bag. There was a smudge of marmalade in the corner of her mouth and I licked my thumb before aiming for the sugar-syrup. She dodged me before I could get there though. 'Do not put that anywhere near me,' she rubbed a hand across her lips, 'that's disgusting.'

'You're disgusting,' I joked, 'get out of the house.'

I unlocked the car for her to clamber in while I locked up. Since Theo left us, I took a great measure of care when it came to locking doors, windows, setting alarms. But when we moved here some years back – when Jessica was just a twinkle in my eye, still – part of the appeal had been that somehow this particular neighbourhood had remained a safe one, even with the grit-grime of the world around us. Safe like, suspiciously low crime rates; safe like, people often didn't even bother locking their front doors, if they weren't going far. But despite what Jessica thought regarding our strong and independent status – 'Who would dare even try it? We're Alphas!' – it *was* just us, and you couldn't be too careful.

Jessica was already fiddling with the Bluetooth settings when I got in the car.

'Put your belt on,' I said as I climbed in.

'I will in a seco–'

'Put your belt on.'

The hum of the engine was the only sound for a second then, while she reached behind her shoulder to grab the belt. When I heard the click of it, I knocked the car into gear. 'Now you can mess around with music.'

'Thank God, because yours is…' She petered out and made a flabber-flubber noise by rolling her lips. I let the dig slide, but when the deep thrum of a drumbeat started to shudder through the doors and floor of the car, it took some self-control to bite back on a rebuttal. Instead, though, I only smiled and let my daughter have the win. It was a good morning, I decided, I felt it in my belly; right in the pit, where my three mouthfuls of good coffee were sloshing around.

'What's your plan for the day?' she asked as we pulled into the queue for the school gates. Music choice aside, Jessica was a good kid, really. How many other seventeen-year-olds gave a shit about their mother's plans for a Wednesday?

I looked out of my window and spotted the football field. It was wearing the same winter-tog thickness that our own garden had been failing to shrug off. But there were already the early bird kids – the someday sports scholarships – running their laps through the mist.

'I think I'm going to see your dad.'

Theo hated flowers. Before, I would limit my flower deliveries to special occasions and sad days – because they were the perfect accompaniment to both. Since, I bought flowers on any occasion: special; sad; Tuesdays. But I never brought them with me when I visited him. Instead, I stopped on the way to buy a bag of salted pretzels – his favourite snack – and a packet of tissues. I used the first one to wipe clean the seasonal grime that clung to his headstone. I even dampened the outline of the writing with a licked thumb and drew his name clear – and I thought of our daughter recoiling at the gesture only twenty minutes ago.

I laughed. 'She's turned into such a teenager. You'd love it.' I took off my waterproof and laid it on the ground in front of his plot, then I sat down cross-legged in front of him. The pretzel bag made a noise that was too loud for the churchyard when I yanked it open and I looked around to see if any other visitors were giving evil eyes at the sound or its maker, like you might in a cinema screening. But I was the only person there. The fog had started to lift, but slowly, and I wondered if anyone arriving would even notice me sitting there, or whether I'd made myself invisible.

That's exactly what I'd wanted, after Theo died. To fold myself into the floorboards of this world and whatever happens after it; to disappear. It had been Freya – lovely, kind, wild Freya, my best friend of nearly eighteen years now – who had shaken me by the shoulders and pointed my glass stare in the direction of Jessica: my seven-year old without a father.

'Thank God for that kid, Theo, I'm telling you.' I smiled and placed a single pretzel on the ground in front of the headstone. 'Right, where to start…'

I told him how well Jessica was doing at school; though I felt like a broken record for it. Jessica was *always* doing well at school. Since university was first mentioned at the start of her A-levels, there'd been a neat ball of fire sitting under her backside driving her to do more, be better, push harder. I was one of the few sixth-form mothers telling their kid to ease off the gas rather than press down on it that bit more. 'I don't know which one of us she gets that from.' I laughed, because of course, it was both of us. Then I told him about Freya, and how worried she was because Ryan isn't as driven as he could be. 'But I think that's Freya being hard on him, mostly. You know what she's like.' Then we came to my work, where nothing much had changed, and I remained in the slow but steady world of academic content work. 'I'm writing a textbook about a subject I know nothing about,' I threw another pretzel in my mouth and laughed around the crunch, 'and yes, it's still wild that people let me do this for a living.' Theo had watched me shift from one topic to another over the years, becoming an expert in everything and nothing all at once – but the pay was good and my work attire typically consisted of soft-touch lounge pants from Primark, which had always felt like a perk. 'I think we're going to Freya's for Christmas this year rather than her coming to us,' I rabbited on. 'She's trying to dodge having Kaleb's tribe over and I feel like Jess and I are a good excuse for them not visiting. Not that they don't want to see us…' I talked and talked and Theo listened for nearly a full hour – until the whole bag was empty.

CHAPTER TWO

Freya's front door was a brilliant bright yellow; a subtle indicator of the brilliant bright woman of the house. I'd called her as I was leaving Theo and she'd suggested tea: 'We can set the world right for an hour. Isn't that the best part of a week?' So I'd taken the car home, dropped it on the drive, and walked the five minutes to Freya's house. Her front garden was dotted with dying wildflowers, a sign of the seasons, though there were late-to-the-party sunflowers in one corner, propping each other up and pushing their small faces open towards the clouds. I trod the gravel path to the front door and gave a knock-knock before ringing the bell. I was eyeing up a planter of lavender when the door opened.

'The garden is a state,' she sighed, 'it's on my list.'

I laughed. '*Everything* is on your list.' I leaned in to kiss her cheek then, and she stepped to one side to let me through into the hallway.

'Yes,' she said, closing the door behind me, 'I suppose *everything* is on my list.' From her tone I thought that it was the beginning of a much longer commentary, and I wondered which job Kaleb had neglected to do over the weekend – whether that's what the cup of tea was for. 'Go on through, doll, the kettle is already boiled.'

Jessica and I were a family; close-knit and supportive and all the things a family should be. But whenever I trod the length of Freya's hallway and spotted the pictures – of her and Kaleb, Kaleb and Ryan, Ryan and Freya, Freya and Kaleb – it always caused a terrible stir in me; a tone-deaf musician strumming an out-of-tune guitar in my head, there was a rush of noise and tightening and plucking. There was something missing from my own hallway of memories, and I hated that still.

'Tea or coffee?'

I landed in a chair at the kitchen table. 'Tea, please. Do you know, I made the most perfect coffee this morning and...' I petered out when I heard someone shifting about upstairs. 'Is Kaleb not at work today?'

'Oh, no, no, he is. Thank God. I tell you, after the weekend...' Freya poured boiled water into two mugs and seemed to forget about the end of her sentence. There was a point – in the months after Theo died, when Freya near as damn it held my hand through day-to-day life – when she refused to moan, at all, about Kaleb. I could always tell when he'd infuriated her, though she never wanted to admit it to me, as though my having lost a husband had made her especially grateful to have kept a hold of her own. It was all worsened, too, by the quiet knowledge that Kaleb was meant to have been in the car with Theo, when the accident happened. They were meant to be golfing somewhere together, but Kaleb had work and Theo decided to go still and the other driver just–

'Anyway, less of Kaleb,' she said, setting down the drink in front of me, and I was grateful that she'd interrupted the memory. 'How was Theo?' She flashed a tight smile. 'Everything okay?'

I nodded. 'I just needed to see him, be near him for a minute.'

'Well, that's more than allowed.' She took a seat opposite me and reached over to squeeze my hand. 'What did you want to do for his birthday this year?'

It had, somehow, been ten years since Theo's accident. In those years, Freya and I had always celebrated his birthday in the same way: dinner in his favourite restaurant; a large glass of red at his favourite bar in the city centre; a night at his favourite hotel in the city too. It was an unofficial girls' night away, though we never called it as much because of the morbidity it stirred in the pair of us – unsaid, but I knew Freya well enough to know she felt it too. Still, she was always polite enough to ask what I wanted to do to celebrate, *if* I wanted to celebrate, even though by now we had a rolling reservation everywhere.

'Same as usual. Unless you're bu–'

'I'm never busy.'

'You know what I mean.'

'I do.' She let go and leaned back in her chair. 'But my answer stands.'

'Thank you.' I sipped at my hot tea. 'So what's happening here?'

'Business as usual. Kaleb is at work. He's got a work thing tonight actually, some…' She waved a hand around. 'Oh, Christ, I don't know. Something to do with dentistry.'

I snorted a laugh. 'Well, that checks out.' Kaleb *was* a dentist after all, though I could never make sense of someone so nice doing something quite so grim. 'He doesn't want you to be there?'

'Oh, I'm sure he does. But I'd rather have my teeth pulled out with rusty pliers than spend a night with–'

'People qualified to pull your teeth out with rusty pliers.'

She clicked her fingers. 'Got it in one.' She paused to sip. 'Besides which, I'm up to my eyes in colour palettes and textiles for this new job, so I could really do with spending a decent wedge of today on those mood boards that are clogging up my studio at the minute.' She rubbed hard at her eyes and when she pulled her fingertips away her underlids were smudged with mascara. I didn't say anything. Freya was one of those women who looked better and better the more dishevelled she became over the course of the average day. It was an artist thing; I was sure of it. But either way, she could pull off panda eyes better than any woman I'd ever met. I only smiled into my mug then, and took another sip. 'Do you want to come over tonight?'

'You *just* said you were busy.'

'A girl's gotta eat!'

We shared a laugh that petered out as Ryan walked into the room. The stocky teen smiled and rolled his eyes. 'What are you two hatching?'

'I was just inviting Annie over for dinner tonight.' Freya winked at me over the rim of her mug.

'And the dentist social thing of Dad's...'

'I'd love to go, but I'm having dinner with Annie.'

I leaned forward and slapped her arm. 'I'm not going to be an alibi.'

'It's too late, you've agreed. That's legally binding. Right, Ryan?'

He put his hands up in mock surrender. 'I am not getting involved.'

Kaleb wasn't a bad-looking man by any stretch of the imagination. But Freya was a bloody gorgeous woman. And Ryan was most definitely her son. Even in the kitchen, with his mess of dark blond hair – long, in the way cool boys wore it these days – tangled up in a scrunchie, accompanied by jogging bottoms that were rolled up at the ankles, and his baggy T-shirt that said something about the name of a band I didn't recognise. *Christ, Annie, you got old real fast.* Which is to say, even without trying, he was still a knock-out. And he'd always been a nice kid, too, which I thought must make him an incredibly popular-unpopular-popular boy at school. He made small talk with us both while waiting for the microwave to ping the arrival of his packet noodles. It was during moments like these – gentle, quiet, easy moments – I came to understand how my daughter had fallen so helplessly in love with the boy. Thank God the feeling was mutual.

Jessica and Ryan were a whole three days apart from each other in age. Freya and I had met on the maternity ward when *both* our husbands had been caught short at work and couldn't make our respective appointments. We'd instantly bonded over stretch marks and food cravings – then found out we only lived a single street away from each other. We were inseparable for the rest of our pregnancies – and for most of the interim years since, too. Jessica arrived first and, through long and winding phone calls, I told Freya she would be fine with childbirth; if I could do it then she could *definitely* do it, and really, it wasn't all that bad and… I told her all the other lies that every expectant mother wants to hear before they birth a watermelon, and she'd called me a cheating cow for it when she arrived home with a small bundle of baby boy in her arms. It had been an idle daydream for the pair of us that our kids might become a Disney movie and fall in love. But when they were just thirteen, the dream came true. The pair of them herded me, Freya and Kaleb into my living room and shuffled awkwardly from one foot to the other, told us it was important, they were nervous – a whole drawn-out non-explanation. Before eventually Jessica had grabbed Ryan's hand and announced, 'We're in love!'

'Oh,' Ryan pulled a humming phone from his pocket, 'it's Jess.'

It warmed me to see him smiling into the handset. 'Tell her to stop texting in lessons,' I joked.

And Ryan's head snapped up, his eyes wide as though someone were checking his pupil reactions. *What have I done?* I thought as I glanced back at Freya who was frowning. But she soon turned to her son instead.

'In lessons?' Freya looked my way again and I caught a quick headshake from Ryan.

I pressed my fingertips to my forehead. 'What am I like? Of

course, she isn't in lessons.' I laughed. 'You've got that thing today, haven't you, the lot of you...'

'The training, for teachers.'

I clicked my fingers. 'Yes. Christ, honestly, I'd forget my head.' Freya shot me a narrow-eyed look and I felt my stomach clench. *Let it go,* I begged, *please, Freya, let it go.* I'd never been able to lie to her – at least, not well. 'So what time shall I come over tonight?' I downed what was left of my tea and flashed a tight smile.

Freya tilted her head, and I hoped she was weighing up an answer to my question, rather than trying to decide whether to push an interrogation. She eventually said, 'Around six, sound okay? Pizza?'

'Perfect.'

'It'll be just us.' She nodded behind her. 'This one is out.'

'Painting the town red?' I asked, and Ryan let out a nervous laugh.

'More like baby pink.'

Which of course, only started Freya off talking about colour palettes and mood boards and... I made a hasty exit for home on the pretext of having work to do, but I promised to be on time – 'Or, you know, *very* close to on time' – when I came back later. Freya kissed me goodbye and Ryan gave a tentative wave from behind his mother in the doorway. By the time I arrived home, the nervy teen had already texted me; short and sweet, it read only:

Thanks so much Annie :)

I didn't reply. I was nervous of Freya finding a digital trail.

CHAPTER THREE

For the rest of the afternoon I danced back and forth on whether to tell Freya after all. Ryan wasn't my child, obviously, or my responsibility. *But what if this is a regular thing,* I started to wonder, *what if he's flunking out on school at the exact time that it's starting to matter?* His mock results hadn't been brilliant – Freya had admitted that much over a rant and a bottle of wine – but I also thought they'd talked it out and decided on a plan and – *My God, what if he's flunking out and he takes Jessica with him?* It was a selfish motivator, I'll admit. But it was a shove enough for me to do some light investigative work when my daughter rolled in from school. She was muddied and roughed up from an afternoon of sports training that, in her own words, was a 'waste of precious fucking time anyway.'

'That's a tongue you've on you there, missus,' I said, my head ducked while I carried on doodling notes for a new textbook project. We weren't a no swearing household, but even by Jessica's standards – considering her steadfast dislike of anything that tested her limited sporting prowess – it seemed an extreme remark.

'I'm sorry, Mum,' she slammed a kitchen cupboard closed, 'it just turned into a really long… Well, just a pig of a day, that's all.' She was facing away from me, ferreting through the contents of a different cupboard. I couldn't see the exhaustion but I could hear it.

'Why don't I fix you actual dinner, rather than whatever crap you're going to pull out of that sweet box?' She turned around with a mouthful of jelly babies. 'Or you can load up on sugar, also a sensible and wise choice after a pig of a day.'

She laughed around the softness of the jellies. 'What are we having?'

'Well,' I stood, 'I'm having pizza with Freya. You can have…'

'Pizza on my own?'

She's had a pig of a day, I reminded myself. 'Order in, charge my Uber Eats.'

'You're the best.' She faced away from me again then, and sourced *more* sugar, but this time from the fridge, and in drink form. I only shook my head and went back to my scribbling. I hoped it might make my interrogation seem more natural.

'How was Ryan today?'

Of course, I was putting my daughter in an impossible position; of course, I was testing whether she would lie to cover for her boyfriend. But I was also hoping this would crack open a wider conversation, one that might help me to work out how often Ryan was actually cutting classes – and anything else that he shouldn't have been doing. Besides which, Jessica had never had a game face for lies – she took after me in that respect – so I'd softened my guilt by at least waiting until she was facing away from me; I gave the kid a fighting chance.

But there was a long and heavy pause before she said, 'You already know he wasn't in school today, Mum.'

I heaved out a sigh. 'You're a good kid, Jess.'

'So is he,' she answered as she turned, drink in hand.

Under the table I lifted a leg to kick out the chair opposite me, and she took the cue. She was guzzling down a tall glass of Pepsi when I asked, 'Is he doing this a lot?'

She shifted her head side to side. 'I don't know whether I'd say *a lot*.'

'More than once?'

A sad laugh tumbled out of her, nearly a huff. 'Yes, more than once.'

'Weekly?'

'Mum, isn't this a conversation to have... Wait, no. This *isn't* a conversation to have. It's between him and *his* mum.' She arched an eyebrow. 'And you know I'm right.'

'Nice try, but his mum happens to be my best friend. Do I need to be talking to Freya about this?'

She downed the rest of her drink and I wondered whether she was buying time. 'Honestly? I don't know. Ryan... he's going through something, I think. Well, I know. I just don't know what it is.'

'Then how do you know he's going through something at all?'

She smiled. 'I just know.'

In that second, my daughter felt less like a child and more like a young woman who knew her boyfriend too well, and there was a twirl-tumble-spin of something in my belly that made me tilt my head and eye her differently. She was so much like her father sometimes.

'Okay, well is *that* something I should be talking to Freya about?'

She leaned back in her chair. 'To say what? My worry-wart daughter thinks there's something wrong with your son because he isn't as keen as he used to be?'

Ah. I matched her gesture, leaned back from the table and avoided eye contact. 'Is that what this is actually about?'

'Mum...'

'I'm not pushing,' I held my hands up in a defensive gesture, 'but we're already talking about it, so we may as well get everything out at once rather than stop-start-stop over the next… I don't know, however many weeks or months or… You think Ryan has lost interest?'

Jessica tilted her head from one side to the other and back, and I imagined the slide-clatter of marbles; small ideas rushing around. 'It's just whatever it is he's going through, right? I mean, he hasn't *said* he's lost interest. We're still talking about future choices and, like, even on days when he isn't in school, we're still talking and texting and stuff. So he can't have *lost*-lost interest? I think he's just a bit cooler than he was because of all the shit he isn't talking to me about, I just… I just don't know what I'm meant to do, exactly, without knowing what the stuff is.'

I left a beat of quiet before I moved to answer but Jessica unhinged her jaws to let more feeling out, and I wasn't about to cut her off. 'I love him and he's my best friend and I can *always* tell when something is wrong. This is just the first time that like, I don't know, he hasn't wanted to talk to me about whatever it is and… I trust him, I just worry that whatever is going on must be bad for him not to tell me.' She huffed a laugh. 'Or maybe what's actually happening is that he's got exactly the same exam, university, life worries that I've got and I'm just more vocal about the whole thing while he's more of a keep-himself-to-himself person.'

Oh, I smiled at my girl and thought, *to be seventeen and have life worries.* Though I also found myself questioning her phrasing; I hadn't ever thought of Ryan as a keep-himself-to-himself type of young man. From a dot he'd been bold and brazen and outlandish. But then – I sipped my lukewarm tea to buy myself a second – people change; especially teenagers.

'I won't tell Freya anything.'

Jessica heaved out a sigh of relief. 'Thank you, Mum.'

'But I do think that you should talk to Ryan about all of this.' I could see the reservation in the expression she flashed, so I reached across to grab her hand, gently squeeze. 'You're a kind and mature young woman for being astute to your partner's needs. He'll appreciate that, if not now, then certainly a few years down the line when he wishes for someone to magically know what he's thinking.'

'None of that,' she waved a hand around as though gesturing to words strung out between us, 'sounds sexy to me.'

I snorted. 'Well, that's a whole different conversation.' I stood from the table and crossed behind her, but sneaked a kiss onto the crown of her head as I passed. 'And frankly not one that I'm prepared to have.'

'Thank God because I think I actually would die.'

'You and me both, kid.' I dropped my cup into the sink. 'You and me both.'

It was only Freya's, but it was as close as I got to a night out. So I layered on foundation, then blusher; used a lip pencil, then drew on my smile; then did my best impression of a dumbstruck goldfish while I flicked my eyelashes into a high volume curl that I would regret later, on discovering, no doubt, that my make-up wipes were powerless against the black liquid. Still, I felt pretty when I looked in the mirror at the end of it all. Though I soon shrugged at my use of the word. *Maybe not pretty,* I decided as I snapped off the bathroom light, *but certainly passable.* I wasn't altogether convinced that I'd felt pretty since the morning of Theo's accident. He, true to form, had kissed my cheek and called me beautiful and pinched my arse as I set his morning tea on the bedside table. It had been a long and hilarious conversation with Jessica some four years earlier when Theo had had to explain to her that the arse-pinching was a Mummy and Daddy thing, rather than a Polite Hello to your Nursery Teacher thing – which was where Jessica had made her first social faux pas. I'd rolled the story out on her fourteenth birthday in front of Ryan; it had been a memory that Theo and I had agreed to back-pocket until Jess first brought a boy home.

By the time I was walking downstairs – in slim-fit jeans and a loose-fit linen shirt, in light blue to try to counteract the grey outdoors – I was laughing so hard at the influx of memories that Jessica shot me an arched eyebrow when I arrived in front of her. She'd been peering through the front-door window.

I reached forward to touch her cheek. 'Nothing to bother about, lovely girl. Waiting on Ryan?'

'What? No, pizza.' She looked through the window again. 'The app said the guy would be here by now and I could eat a mouldy horse.'

'Well, on that tender note.' I reached behind her and pulled my coat free from its hook. 'I won't be late but I will be drunk. Take your house keys and be sure to lock up behind you when you go anywhere.'

'Mm-hmm, whatever you say.'

She was too busy looking through the window again to give me anything more in response. I tapped her out of the way to open the front door, pecked her cheek – and left behind the ghost of a red mouth print – then squeezed free of the house. Though something didn't feel quite right, slinking off to get drunk on a school night while my daughter waited at home for a man – the role reversal that I imagined every mother must dread.

CHAPTER FOUR

It took three attempts for me to check the time on my phone screen when I woke up the following morning – because of course, a quiet night at Freya's with a few glasses of wine could *never* be just that. When I'd arrived there were already two bottles parked on the table, and Freya told me that pizza was a good hour away.

'How the hell is it an hour away?' I'd asked. 'Jess just got hers in lightning speed while I was on my way here.'

She'd poured a large glass of red and pushed it along the table to me. 'Well, to start with, I haven't ordered it yet.'

From there, the laughter started. I could remember joking and moaning in equal measure about our respective jobs – she'd told me about a recent client who only wanted different shades of yellow around her house, and had threatened to give Freya the push entirely when she'd tried to sneak a beige rug into the utility room – and from there we talked about the kids, their relationship to each other, and then to the world, and then – I groaned and rubbed at my forehead where a dull thud appeared every time I tried to move.

'I just worry about Ryan,' she'd said, uncorking the second bottle when we were two-thirds of the way through the first. 'Do you think he'll be okay?'

'In life?' I'd raised an eyebrow, playfully, to try to soften the mood.

'No, arse, in university. Well, in life, too, but in university specifically. I mean, do you think he'll get there? The way he is at the minute…'

I'd bitten my tongue then, and said nothing of Jessica's suspicions. It was clear that Freya had her own reservations about her son, too, but I'd wagered that half a bottle of wine and an empty stomach weren't the ideal conditions to have at play in my talking to her about it. So instead I'd only grabbed her hand and said, 'Ryan is a good kid, my lovely, you've raised him right. Whatever happens with his exams, it'll all work out. These things do.' I'd winked and downed the rest of my drink to keep my mouth busy then, and in the split second that I came up for air, the doorbell had sounded. 'If that's the delivery man then I'll kiss him square on the mouth for that food.'

Freya had howled with laughter at that and shouted, 'It would be about bloody time,' after me as I'd rushed down the hallway.

I turned over in bed and stared at the empty side of the mattress. There hadn't been anyone there since Theo, and during our worst conversations Freya often made a 'use it or lose it' joke where she suggested the least I could be doing was having a fling. During our best conversations, she kindly offered to set me up, or help with dating apps or– My stomach rolled over in a small tsunami at the mere thought of it. *Though that might be the wine,* I thought then, swallowing back the sting of acid that lined my throat. I really needed to move, to get coffee, or water at least. But instead, I stretched my hand to the cold side of the bed and decided I could give myself a minute longer, to enjoy the morning quiet with my ghost of a husband.

I remembered then, in a hand-clap instant, something else Freya had spoken about the night before. *Was that when the second bottle was open, or was it a third?* I tried to clear the memory.

'Freya thinks Kaleb might be having a fling with someone at work.' I spoke to the hollow space. I did this sometimes; spoke as though Theo were there. Years ago, when I still thought grief counsellors were useful, I'd confided this habit to the woman I'd been speaking to about my loss. That was how she always referred to it; as though I'd shed the weight of something. I had in many ways, I suppose: I'd shed a whole thirteen and a half stones when Theo had died. She'd told me that it was normal, to still speak to a spouse as though they were there; she said some people did it their whole lives after, and that thought was as disturbing as it was comforting. I'd stopped seeing her shortly after that talk. It wasn't that she wasn't helpful, of course. She was, in the early days especially, but sooner or later you have to accept that counsellors are counsellors and not, in fact, magicians.

I wedged my hand between the two pillows at the head of the bed on Theo's side and closed my eyes. 'She doesn't think it's his receptionist, said he's not cliché enough for that, but she reckons there's someone. I told her she was being a daft cow, obviously, and that Kaleb loves her, because that's what you're meant to say to these things, isn't it? But I don't know. Would I even be able to tell if he were having a fling? Am I qualified to judge?'

I huffed out a harsh laugh and spoke in a lower voice. 'I hadn't been able to tell when you had...'

I screwed my eyes tighter and tried to force away the memory before it could gain traction. It was a long time ago, I reminded myself, and there was no sense in being angry about it now. After all, I hadn't known the woman, and Theo had been dead for ten years. *Who am I even supposed to be angry with now?*

The cold comfort of the pillow and the blank space of the

sheets lost its appeal then, and I braved moving. I eased myself round to the edge of the bed and slowly, *slowly*, shifted into an upright position. The dull thud in my head became more pronounced and I added soluble aspirin to my list of reasons to get up – after a shower, a long one, and I deliberately chose a body wash that promised to be refreshing. Though when I trod down to the kitchen some fifteen minutes later, I couldn't say that I felt any more refreshed than I had to begin with. Radox probably had its limits.

'But then, it didn't say anything about red wine consumption on the bottle,' I said to myself as I flicked the kettle to boil and grabbed one of the larger mugs that was hanging on the steel tree on the kitchen worktop. My laptop was already waiting for me from the day before, with research papers scattered around it, as though I were an ill-prepared teenager on the eve of an exam. But instead of booting up the machine I opted to stare longingly into the garden. 'A much better use of my time.' Everything was dew-wet and nearly crisp in the turn of the weather. Winter wasn't even in full bloom yet and somehow the whole season had shifted sideways since we hit mid-October. I wondered whether there were even traces of a frost out there. I wrapped myself in a hug and rubbed at my arms, feeling suddenly like the cold had seeped into me, then I turned back to the task at hand.

I made coffee and put bread in to toast, then I tackled the battle of the laptop. I was grateful for every slight interruption though: the slow whir of updates as my machine tried to bring itself round; the chirp of my phone that turned out to be another friend inviting me for drinks that evening. Honestly, it was beginning to feel like since our teenagers became late-teenagers, we'd all somehow regressed to our younger selves. I was far from being the worst mum of the bunch, not through lack of trying on the part of my friends, and even with a hangover I toyed with typing *Oh, go on then!* before I eventually tapped out *Another time, lovely, I'm busy tonight.* The toaster sprang to life then, too, but midway through moving to it I heard a shift in the house. My stomach made the same wave-roll-tumble as it had earlier, only this time it wasn't the alcohol; only a slight worry. It had become a bigger concern as the years rolled by, that we mightn't be safe in the house, somehow, without Theo here. Not that Theo had been the great defender or anything but–

There came another groan of movement.

I glanced at the wall clock to see whether there was an error on my part, thinking my blurry eyes might have spotted the wrong time earlier. But no, Jessica should have left for school a good hour ago. And yet...

'Jess?'

Nothing. So I tried again, louder. 'Jessica, is that you?'

When the third shift of movement came, though, I was convinced it was the corner of the house where Jessica's room was. I grabbed my phone from the kitchen table – *always be ready to call someone, anyone* – and moved through the hallway towards the stairs. Then serendipity struck: my phone hummed to life in my hand and the caller ID showed Kaleb. *What can you want?*

I thought about not answering, thought of dealing with one crisis at a time; especially given that Kaleb's crisis was probably a jovial one, something about the state Freya was in this morning, or maybe even last night when he'd eventually arrived home. *That's right, he'd been out* so *late, hadn't he?* I struggled to prioritise thoughts while I lingered at the bottom of the staircase, staring upwards as though waiting for a silhouette monster to appear. When the call rang off, to voicemail, I thought the decision was made for me. But I hardly got a foot on the bottom step when Kaleb started to call again.

I clicked to accept. 'Look, whatever horrid hangover your wife might–'

'Annie, can you come up to the house?' Kaleb's voice was a flat tyre; deflated and thick with... something.

'What's going on?'

'I just need… We need for you to come up to the house.'

'Kaleb, I'm… I think Jess is here. Let me just check and then… Is Freya okay? Did something happen?'

There came a long pause before he answered. 'It's Ryan.'

I sank under the weight of his name. Without anything more, I somehow knew what had happened. Not the circumstances, of course, only the end.

'Kaleb, I… I don't… Oh God.' I rested my forearms on my thighs and dropped my head. Selfishly – *Is this selfish?* – I thought of Jessica; Jessica, who may well be sleeping upstairs; Jessica who was readying to take exams and be a grown-up and step out into the world; Jessica who was making plans with– 'What happened?'

'Can you just come to the house, please? Freya needs… We both need you.'

I didn't know how to fill the empty space that followed. Everything started to hurt then, physically ache as though I'd been through a spin class without proper prep and I tried hard to swallow down the swill of sick I could feel shifting in my stomach and– 'Please bring Jessica, if Jessica is… Bring her, would you?'

'Of course.' I forced myself up. 'Of course, I'll check and get her, and then we'll be there. Of course we'll be there.'

Kaleb disconnected the call without anything more and I sat on that bottom step for what felt like a long time. But when I checked my phone again only a minute at most had rolled by. I wondered, like the shocked and bereaved often do, whether something odd had happened then. I entertained the optimistic possibility that the intricacies of scientific discovery really were onto something, which might mean time loops really were real. And if so, perhaps this wasn't our *real* time loop at all but a strange and mangled one, unsteady on its science feet, where time moved in a different way and bad things happened but they didn't *really* happen, if we could only get back to– I pinched my left wrist hard enough to bruise. A bad thing had happened. And for the second time in her short life, I was going to have to sit down with my daughter and snatch a loved one away. It would be a wonder if someday she didn't hate me.

CHAPTER FIVE

The door was already partway opened and I knew, then, that it must have been Jessica shifting about upstairs that I'd heard. What I didn't know was why she was there, why she wasn't at school already – but the importance of that fell down the edges of the gaping hole I was about to split open in her world. She was in bed still, and faced away from the door. There was a small creak as I pushed into the room and I hoped the noise might rouse her but it didn't. Instead, I had to sit on the edge of her bed, and I had to lay a hand on her hunched form, and I had to–

'Sweetheart,' I spoke softly and accompanied it with a weak nudge. But when she didn't respond my hand tensed and the movement became something firmer. 'Jessica, I need for you to wake up for me, sweetheart. Can you…' I shook, gently, like I might have done when she was a child and I was rocking her to sleep, and the comparison made a swell of tears form that I had to try especially hard to hold back. I felt my throat constrict and I was worried then, that the words, the formal announcement it was my job to make – all over again, just as I had with Theo – mightn't be able to force its way out.

'What's going on?' She rolled over and I searched her for signs of sickness. I couldn't understand why she was here. Though in many ways I was thankful we were having this conversation here, rather than in front of a common room full of students. *But you're about to taint the place with this,* I thought, *you're about to make her bedroom a tomb.* And I tried very hard to remember where she'd been when I told her about Theo. *Were we here,* I thought back, *or did someone bring Jessica to Freya's?*

'Sweetheart, sit up for me.'

She followed the instruction though it looked like an effort for her.

'Are you okay?' she asked.

'Sweetheart, Kaleb just called me.' I couldn't be sure of it, but I thought I felt something in her tense then, and I wondered whether she was bracing for bad news already. 'Ryan... There's been some kind of accident, sweetheart, I think, I don't know the details yet. But we need to go to Freya's house, okay?'

'What about Ryan, Mum?'

I puckered my lips and pulled in a deep breath. 'Sweetheart, he's... something happened, I don't know what... Kaleb, he called and said we need to go to the house. We need...' I petered out when I saw her expression. It was steel cold and steadfastly fixed to a spot on the duvet. 'Sweetheart?' I gently shook again. 'Sweetheart, what happened last night? When you left Ryan, where was he?'

She looked at me then, but she was startled, as though snapping out of a trance. 'I didn't see Ryan last night.'

'But when I left, I told you... You said...' I tried to remember. What had she said? 'I told you to take your house keys if you went anywhere.'

'And I didn't. I was here all night, Mum. I tried...' She rubbed hard at her face and a choked noise fell out of her, and I wondered whether her words were lodged too. 'I tried to get hold of Ryan but I couldn't, so I stayed here. I ate pizza and... Fucking hell, I was eating pizza...'

I waited for the tears to come but they didn't form. Instead, she fell silent and stared again at the spot on the duvet. And I explained another two times that we needed to go, we needed to leave. 'Jessica, we need to not be here.'

I walked with an arm around my daughter the same way a nurse might guide a patient in recovery. My right arm was wrapped around her, my hand cupped against her shoulder; my left hand gently pressed to her left upper arm. She took slow and unsteady steps and she asked no questions, and I hated the level of trust she was putting in me, when I was only guiding her towards something that would devastate her. I imagined an accident that triggered mis-memories of cars colliding, leftover re-imaginings from Theo's own accident with another driver; another driver, who also didn't escape the crash. What other kind of accident was there for a teenage boy to fall victim to? There must have been many answers to that question. But while I was trying to keep my daughter upright, keep my own body steady, hold my stare straight ahead to the road we would soon turn into, the only thought I could consider was crushed metal and discarded gears and shattered glass.

We rounded the corner into Freya's road and saw the early evidence of whatever the accident was: a single police car parked immediately outside their front door. It was blocking in Freya and Kaleb's cars, and Ryan's own clapped-out Corsa. *So it wasn't a crash,* was the first thought that came to me and I found a sigh of relief escaped, though I wasn't sure why. *It's still an accident,* I reminded myself, *whatever has happened, Ryan is still–*

'Mum, Mum, I can't do this,' Jess managed, the words knocking against her teeth to cause a stutter that made her seem even more childlike. She physically recoiled, and pulled free of my grip in the process. 'I can't do this. I can't… I can't be here for this, for whatever is about to happen.'

'I know, my darling girl, I know.' I yanked her back towards me to hold her close, though I was painfully aware that that must mean she could see the police vehicle from her view over my shoulder. 'Whatever has happened, whatever… It's best that we know, sweetheart, okay? It's best that we hear it now.' She said nothing, only jutted her small chin against my shoulder as she nodded. 'Whatever has happened…' I started to say again, though it dawned on me that there was no new end to that sentence; there was nothing easy ahead.

The walk from one end of Freya's road to the other had never seemed so long. We were midway into the cul-de-sac when I realised I was also beginning to shake, though I tried to steady it against Jess's vibrations that seemed to become more pronounced the closer we came to the property. This house had been a haven in the hardest of times, but it was also the sweet jar where we stored some of the best family memories; some of which featured Theo, even, but most of which featured Ryan. And my belly audibly groaned at the thought of overwriting that information with whatever horror lay behind the door now. I almost didn't want to knock against Freya's yellow paintwork; I didn't want to tarnish the brightness of their home. *But something already has,* I thought as I tapped my knuckles against the door, before returning my grip on Jessica. I kissed the side of her temple while we waited, but I didn't offer any reassurances. I wasn't prepared to lie to her while we waited for an official body to tell us what had happened to her–

The front door was yanked open with a force.

'Kaleb, what the hell has–'

He fell forwards and pulled us both into a hug. It was a short and rough embrace, though he paused to kiss Jessica's forehead as he pulled away. 'I'm so, so sorry, Jessie, just so… so fucking sorry.'

Without waiting for a reply he moved back into the house and there seemed no other option but to tread the path he'd paved for us. I put Jessica ahead of me, but held on to her on either side of her ribs as though to steady her, in case the incoming blow were to collapse her entirely. I closed the front door behind us and looked up to see Kaleb lingering in the doorway of the living room; his palm was pressed flat against his mouth while he listened to whatever was being listed out inside the space proper, and I wondered whether a sob lay behind his hand – or whether, when it eventually came, it would be something more guttural. A scream might erupt, an animal sound; something howling with the loss of young.

Jessica and I swapped places in the hallway so I could reach Kaleb. But when I met him at the door I caught sight of Freya inside, sitting on the sofa with a police officer crouched in front of her. She looked like a creature from a horror film; black rivers running down each cheek, her eyes bloodshot, her hair mangled from shaking hands having run through it so many times.

'It's the third time they've explained it to her,' Kaleb said quietly.

I set my palm flat against the space between his shoulder blades. 'Explained what, Kaleb?'

He turned to me with a shocked expression. 'Oh, oh, of course, I didn't–'

'He's really dead, isn't he?' Jessica's small question came from behind us both.

'Is that Jess? Is Jessica here?' Freya pushed past me and made her way towards my daughter, and I saw Jess recoil. Her back was pressed flat against the front door by the time Freya reached her. 'Doll.' She pulled her into a hug though Jessica's body remained rigid and I hated this, I hated it all. I hated that Ryan was–

'I think they think he was murdered.' Kaleb spoke in a near

whisper next to me. My head snapped around at the announcement. 'Not murdered, murder is planned, isn't it?' he asked, and he seemed to be looking at me in anticipation of an answer. 'Isn't that right?'

'I... I don't...'

'Kaleb, can you show me where things are in the kitchen?' It was an alien voice asking the question; the officer, the one who'd been re-explaining to Freya when we arrived, she was guiding Kaleb away from me then, and I wanted to reach out a hand to latch onto him, but she seemed so confident in the action and she was the police so they must know, and I tried to order everything in my head before I opened my mouth but–

'Can someone tell us what the fuck is happening?'

The officer reappeared and wrapped an arm around my shoulder then. She cradled me how I had cradled my daughter on the walk there, and I felt myself crumple into the woman. She turned me towards the living room and directed me – 'Just in here, miss, that's right.' – and from my side vision I could see that Freya and Jessica were following. Freya encouraged Jess along, though, while Jessica dragged and shuffled her feet. 'That's it, just take a seat.' When everyone had filed into the room again she spoke, softly, in small sentences. I looked from the woman to Kaleb, propped against – or propped up by, perhaps – the doorframe, and I looked at Freya who was cradling my daughter; Jessica, who had the same glass-eyed stare. And then I looked back at the woman who was still speaking, still saying something about a body, and the school's football field and–

'At this time we're treating the death as suspicious.'

CHAPTER SIX

In the two days afterwards, I made one hundred and four cups of tea across five people. I took 53,000 steps as I ran between the two houses. And I completed too many other inane but countable tasks to keep my mind occupied and away from the fire; the burning knowledge that something terrible had happened, and to one of our babies. Once the information finally settled with me, Freya asked if we could move in – 'I just want you both so, so close, where I can keep an eye on you.' – but Jessica couldn't stand to be in their house. When I floated the suggestion with her, she looked at me as though I'd slapped her.

'I can't be in his room, Mum, I can't be in… I can't stand to be in that house…'

There were too many memories; cobwebs of recalled information that stretched out in the corners of every room, and there was nothing I could do to sweep them away for her. Instead, I lived between the houses; an hour here, an hour there, and whenever the family liaison officer arrived – which was often, for short bursts sometimes, but for longer stretches of the day, too – I excused myself to check on my girl.

Towards the end of that second day when I got home, the

house had such an eerie silence about it that I wondered whether she'd gone out. I locked the door behind me and cocked an ear in the direction of the stairs, to listen out for the rush of a bathroom tap or the shift of her turning in bed. There was nothing.

I couldn't stand the thought of making another cup of tea – one that would invariably go too cold to drink anyway, because there wasn't much that I could stand the thought of eating or drinking – but still, I gravitated towards the kitchen. It was where the biggest of discussions had happened: career talks with my daughter; confessions from my husband; conversations with clients for work and–

'Sweetheart.' Jessica was faced away from the doorway; she stood directly in front of the sink, staring into the stretch of garden ahead of her. The sun was sinking and there was little light left to see anything through, but still she stayed focused straight ahead as though she hadn't even heard me. 'Sweetheart,' I tried again, 'I didn't realise you were here. I thought... I thought you might have gone out.' When I rounded to catch a glimpse of her face, I saw that she was holding a mug. She had a hand clasped either side, like she was trying to warm herself. 'You can click the heating on when I'm not here, Jess, you don't have to wait.'

She shook her head and looked at me then, as though rising from a trance. 'What?'

I nodded at the drink. 'You look like you're cradling a fire.'

'Oh.' She glanced down and shook her head again then. 'No, I...' She set the drink on the counter. 'I think it's cold anyway. It was warm milk. I thought it might help me to sleep, or... I don't know.' She spoke in a slow and drawn-out way that made it sound like she didn't need help in getting to sleep at all, but rather, some helping with coming around. 'I just wanted to drift off for a while.'

'I can understand that.' I stood alongside her and looked out at her view. 'It isn't quite as pretty out there now, is it?' I said, meaning, of course, now the summer flowers had wilted and the grass was damp and an evening fog was rolling in. But somehow when she answered – 'I don't think anything is anymore, Mum.' – it became clear we were both talking about something else.

'Shall I fix you something to eat?'

'How's Freya?' she asked, as though I hadn't posed my own question first.

I didn't know how to answer. In fact, I wasn't sure anyone had coined a word that was big enough, nor bad enough, to explain how Freya was. So instead I said, 'She's as well as can be expected.' Which felt truthful, at least.

'Kaleb?'

'The same, sweetheart.'

'Are the police there?'

'The FLO is, yes. That's why I thought I'd come back here, see if there was anything I could do for you.' I moved away and started to rifle through cupboards behind her. 'I know you won't want anything, sweetheart, but it's important to try to keep your strength up. Can I fix you just a little something? How about beans on toast, something easy?'

There was a long pause before she answered. 'I wish it had been me.'

I froze, midway to reaching for a tin. 'Jessica, you don't mean th–'

'I do, Mum. I wish it had been me.'

I didn't correct her again. I could remember the days after the crash, when information slowly trickled down about the way Theo had died; how much he might have been aware of, while they were trying to cut him out of the vehicle. In those days, I told Freya over and over, 'It should have been me, it should have been me in that fucking car.' Though I realised it was less about wishing it had been me, and more about wishing it had been both of us. I hadn't wanted to go in Theo's place, necessarily – but I would have given anything to have gone along with him.

'Think of Jessica,' Freya had said, every time. 'Think of Jess.'

I had thought of her then, and realised over and over with every howl of my own that even if I wanted to have gone with my husband, I wouldn't have wished it on our daughter. Jessica didn't have an equivalent, though; she didn't have her own young thing to cling to. But it pained me to hear her say it still, in her quiet, little-girl tone. *Think of me*, I wanted to say, *think of me, still living*. But in the days after a heart-wrenching tragedy, who was I to ask her to think of anyone but herself?

'I'm going to make beans on toast.'

Then, without any further acknowledgement, she turned and walked to leave the room. But she paused on the threshold. 'Do they know what happened yet?'

I sucked in a sharp breath. It was accidental; a reflex that I hoped she hadn't noticed. The police had said something about a head wound; something about signs of being choked; something about it being early days. I didn't want to lie to my daughter, but I decided in that moment that I had to. 'Not yet, sweetheart, no. It's still very early days.'

I heard her huff then. 'Is it? It feels like this has already lasted forever.'

Jessica didn't come downstairs again in the thirty minutes that I was home. In the end I left because I realised I needed company too. In the few moments I'd snatched alone it had started to dawn on me – the slow, dawdling fog of a horror sequence – that Ryan had died. *Ryan had been killed,* I tried to correct myself every time but the horror of that, on top of his loss, was too much for my brain to couple up. I trod back towards Freya's then, with a wool ball of guilt at leaving my daughter – but a need not to be alone for any longer either. Though when I rounded the corner to Freya's street, the sight of Freya – greasy hair pulled back into a painfully high ponytail; glasses clinging to the edge of her nose; the sleeves rolled up on what I thought must be one of Ryan's sweatshirts – I wondered what I was about to walk into. I hadn't been expecting anything pleasant, but she looked like…

'Are you about to paint your front door?' I came to a stop at the end of the drive and she turned to look at me.

'What do you think?'

'I think…' I raised my arms and then let them drop to my sides in a defeated gesture. But at machine-fire speed I realised what she was doing then. 'He always hated the colour of this door.'

'Right you are, Annie, right you bloody are.' She turned and went back to stirring paint, as though our exchange were complete.

'Is the FLO still here?' Freya only gestured towards the front door then, which I took to be a yes. 'Don't you want to hear if there are more updates?'

At that, as though pushed by something, she keeled over. She tumbled backwards and landed on her rear, with a leg either side of the paint pot she'd been stirring, and she rested an elbow precariously on each knee – and she sobbed.

'Oh fuck it, Frey, I'm…' I quickly joined her. I sat alongside her with an arm around her back and rocked her as she sobbed. 'I'm sorry, sweetheart, I'm just so sorry.' Any speech that came out of her during that time was inaudible, silenced by the squeaks and the squeals and the gasping for air that came between it all. I wanted to ask whether I'd missed something; whether there *had* been developments, which was why Freya was now sitting outside her home with plans to deface her own front door. But asking any more questions felt like kicking upset that was already waiting to spill, and there was enough of that already. While I held her, I shed my own quiet tears on the top of her head and I hoped she wouldn't feel the dampness of them. But God, how I needed to cry.

Soon, Freya's breathing became steady enough for her to try talking. 'I don't understand who would do this, Annie, I just…' She pulled away so she could turn to face me. 'Ryan never did a single thing wrong in his life. How could he have done? He was a child.'

I thought of him cutting school – the look he'd given me over the top of Freya's head when he thought I might tell her. 'Have the police said anything?'

'That woman…' It took me a second to realise she was referring to the FLO, as though she were The Other Woman in a marriage. 'She's in there talking to Kaleb, she said something about needing Ryan's laptop. The police, they said the other day they'd probably need it. There are other things going, too, I suppose.' She waved her hand around before propping an elbow on her right knee and resting her chin in her palm. She looked utterly hopeless in a way that, if someone had asked me just a week ago, I would have said Freya didn't have it in her to feel. For years, she had been the strong one. I didn't see myself as weak; I only saw Freya as indestructible, unshakeable somehow. Though of course, there's a weak spot in everyone; it had just never crossed my mind that something would come for her child.

'Will you stay here tonight, Ann?' She leaned against me and I was glad she couldn't see my face. 'You can bring Jess, there's so much room and then you wouldn't have to leave and we could… I don't know, we could sit and be heartbroken together, at least.' I felt the jerk of her shoulders, as though she might be trying to laugh, to make light, but it didn't carry through to the tone she'd used. I couldn't blame her for wanting warm bodies under the roof. But Jess wouldn't hear of it; I knew that much without even asking. The mere suggestion of walking along here for a cup of tea earlier in the day had sent her shaking back to the stairs, where she had to sink and compose herself before tackling the climb back to her room. And like a true best friend, Freya guessed at my reservation. 'Jess?'

I sighed. 'She's a shell, Freya. I know she's entitled to be, you all are, *we* all are. I can't even get her to talk, or eat, or… leave the house, by the looks of things. The school called–'

'The bastards, did they?' She snapped upright and I saw a flame of the old Freya. 'About her being off?'

'Yes,' I half-laughed, 'but only to say it wasn't a problem.'

'I should fucking think not. Do you know *no one* from the school has called?'

I wondered whether there was a protocol for this in the teachers' code of conduct for the place. Still, whether or not there was a listed protocol, I was surprised the head hadn't at least passed along his sympathies. *The bastards,* I thought, echoing Freya's judgement, but I tried to keep my expression neutral.

'Late at night, when I'm staring at the ceiling and thinking and pinching myself in the corner of my C-section scar, sometimes, then, I wonder whether anyone cares at all that he's gone.' I opened my mouth to snap a dispute and she set her hand on my arm. 'I don't mean you, I don't mean Jess. Christ, you're running laps between the lot of us and your girl can't leave the house; it's clear you care. But the wider world, everyone outside of us.' She looked upwards then and took a sweep from one side of the sky to the other. 'They'll find something, some sod or another will, something about that time he got drunk, or when that pothead friend of his got expelled. They'll find something and spin it and…' She looked back at me and shrugged. 'What's one more dead kid, Annie? The state the bloody world is in, what's one more…'

CHAPTER SEVEN

The police had forewarned me there would be a visit. Jessica was Ryan's girlfriend; of course they needed to talk to her. Though they hadn't said when they might arrive, only that they would. I realised they were a mere five-minute walk away at any given time, though, so it shouldn't have been a surprise when on the morning of the third day the front doorbell sounded. The detectives weren't what I expected; I suppose there's a lot of television drama to blame for that. For one, they were both much younger. The woman – who introduced herself as DS Victoria Haynes – was, I would guess, not yet forty. She had mouse-brown-blonde hair that was scraped into a messy bun and I wondered whether it was messy, or the kind of messy that Jessica might spend an hour in front of the mirror perfecting before leaving the house with her I-woke-up-like-this appearance. It seemed unlikely that a detective might have that sort of time, but I couldn't be sure. Her eyes were kind but her mouth was set in a line you could balance a spirit level on, and I thought regardless of her hair, the stone face must have been something she worked on for years. Meanwhile her partner – DC Samuel Shaw – was much softer in appearance; he smiled as he introduced himself, held out a hand and, rather than shaking mine, gave me a light squeeze instead. *Had they readied this?* I wondered. *The beginnings of a good-cop-bad-cop routine...* Though that was likely my overexposure to police drama talking, too. After their doorstep introductions, I welcomed them into the house – though welcomed may be a stretch of a term – and saw them into the living room. Jessica wasn't up yet; it had been another evening of night terrors and sweated sheets, and after I'd changed her bedding and dampened her forehead with a cool flannel, I'd left her listening to music in the dark. She said she was fine, that she'd sleep soon. I had no idea whether she'd managed it. I didn't, though, and instead I'd spent much of the night with an ear cocked, listening for the cries of my daughter in the same way I might have done when she was an infant. At least then I would have been able to burp her and nurse her and rock away her worries. *What use am I to her now?*

'I'm afraid Jess isn't up and about yet so you'll have to take her as you find her. She's found all of this incredibly difficult, as you can imagine,' I said, lingering in the doorway while the strangers made themselves comfortable on my two-seater. 'Would you like tea, or coffee? Water?'

They swapped a glance before Haynes answered for the both of them. 'Tea would be lovely, thank you, Annie.' I hadn't told them they could use my first name, and I couldn't decide whether to be irked by it. Though in the aftermath of murder and loss and ugly sensations swarming in and out of me, I was beginning to feel irked by most things in the world.

I excused myself to put the kettle to boil, then on my way back through the hallway I ducked back into the living room. 'I'll just go and wake Jessica.'

'Actually,' Haynes pulled me in, 'we were wondering whether we might talk to you first. If you don't mind? Before we involve Jessica.'

Another swarm of something ran through me; bees, hornets, a

hybrid. A small rumble emerged from the well of my stomach and I tried to remember when, in between forcing food into Jessica and Freya, I'd last eaten anything. 'Of course.' I sat opposite them, sinking into the centre of the three-seater that was only normally used for guests. We were all in the wrong places. 'I'll help however I can, of course.'

Shaw pulled out a notebook. 'We're led to believe you were quite close to Ryan?'

I took a sharp intake of breath when I heard his name. 'Yes, I was.'

'He and Jessica, they grew up together?'

'They were only born days apart. Freya and I, we met at the hospital once when our husbands both stood us up for appointments, and we just clicked and…' I looked from one of them to the other, and suddenly felt self-conscious in my own home. 'You know all of this already, you must do. I'm sorry.'

'Don't apologise.' Haynes had stepped in then. She set a hand flat on her chest. 'I'm a mother, too, I get it. I remember my own other half missing a doctor's appointment and I was so grateful to have other mums around. It's really special, that you and Freya kept in touch like this.' She seemed sincere, but it felt like she'd spread the sympathy too thickly as well. I imagined it as cold toast with thick and full-fat butter; the type you should remove from the fridge at least half an hour before you want to use it. The butter-sympathy clogged and curdled at the edge of the bread, and I suddenly couldn't take her smile seriously. It was too far removed from the stone expression on the woman who had walked in the door not ten minutes ago.

'It is special. We've been lucky to have each other, and the kids have.'

'Freya told us you were a bit of a second mum in lots of ways.' Shaw took control of the conversation again. 'She said she felt Ryan could turn to you if he ever needed anything and she wasn't around.'

I nodded. 'I like to think he felt that way, yes.' Then I remembered the day of– *What do I call it now?* It was no longer the day I went to Freya's for pizza and wine and whine. Now, it was: the last day I saw Ryan alive. I thought of how he'd lied to his mother, how he panicked when he thought I might out him; how he said something – *Or did* I *say something?* – about painting the town pink that same evening. 'Ryan was a good kid,' I added then, but they looked at me like maybe they didn't believe me.

'We've been into Ryan's school already, to have a quick chat with his teachers and his academic coach there.' Haynes let the statement hang for a second before she added, 'It looks as though Ryan had been skipping some classes recently.'

It felt as though she knew that I knew, but I couldn't work out how that might be the case. Still, this was an opportunity, I realised, and it was better to take it now than backtrack to it later. I sucked in a greedy breath and spoke to the floor. 'Ryan *was* skipping classes, that much I know.' It felt as though I'd betrayed someone's trust with the admission – but was it Ryan's, or Jessica's?

'Do you know why?' Shaw asked, pen poised and ready.

'I actually don't, no. I'm not even sure how long it had been going on either. He didn't speak to me about it, at all, I only know it was happening because I caught him in a lie.' Haynes narrowed her eyes at the comment so I continued. 'It was the day,' I gestured with one hand to fill the blank of the sentence and I hoped they might know what I meant. 'I stopped in at Freya's on my way back from visiting my... from visiting my husband's grave. Ryan was at home, and when his phone pinged with a message from Jessica, I said something...' I pressed my fingers to my forehead and tried to dislodge the memory of what I'd actually said. *But does it matter* that *much?* Of course it did, I decided. Not for the police records, though, but for my own: it was the last time Ryan and I had spoken, bar the thank-you message that came later in the day – the one that I'd ignored.

'Pink,' I remembered, though it was a sample from a different part of the conversation, 'he said something about painting the town pink, when I asked if he was painting the town red that night. When he said Jessica had texted, I told him to tell her to get back to classes and Freya, she asked what I meant about classes, because Ryan had told her it was an inset day, or training, whatever it is they call it now. Ryan had lied to his mum, either way. It was a normal day at school, he'd just told her it wasn't.' A sad sigh fell out of me; a defeated huff, more than anything, and I realised then, that was exactly how I felt in the face of all this: defeated. I could do nothing to help the ones I loved most in the world, and it was a terrible, ugly place in which to live.

'Take your time, Annie,' Haynes said then, sensing the struggle. This laboured recollection must have been nothing in comparison to some of the conversations she'd had with Freya. 'Did you talk to Ryan after that?'

'When I got home, he'd texted me to say thank you.'

Shaw looked up from his notetaking. 'Thank you?'

I nodded, but it was Haynes who completed the memory. 'For not telling his mum.'

'I should have,' I said then. 'If I had–'

'It wouldn't have made a difference, Mum.'

My head snapped around at the intrusion. Jessica was slumped in the doorway, wearing a jumper I recognised as Ryan's. She had the sleeves pulled down over her hands and the hood bunched up around her neck; it must have been two sizes too big for her. Her hair was wet, but I hadn't heard the shower pump kick in. *But then,* I looked back at the detectives, *you've kept me distracted.* I felt a flicker of annoyance that they'd pulled me away from duties for so long and I wondered how Freya was too.

'Now might be a good time for me to make that tea,' I said, standing.

'Do you mind having a chat with us, Jessica?' Haynes asked, as

I moved to leave the room. 'It won't take long. We just have some questions about Ryan, if that would be okay.'

I looked up in time to catch Jessica's small head shake. Her eyes were exhausted, glass-like and full to the brim; it wouldn't take long for more tears to spill out. I held her by the shoulders and kissed her forehead. 'I'll only be next door.' It felt like throwing her into a lion's den but it was a necessary evil, too. If not now, then there would be another time. This wasn't exactly going to go away on its own.

In the kitchen I set the kettle to boil again and arranged four mugs on the side. Jess wouldn't drink hers, but I knew she'd cradle its warmth. The lack of food was making her feel the cold and, I thought, probably adding to the lethargy. But there was only so much I could get the girl to eat. I arranged five different types of biscuits on a plate then, as though that might tempt her; besides which, it kept me busy while I waited for the water to boil. When it still hadn't, though, I moved quietly back to stand just outside the living-room doorway: far enough away that my daughter could speak freely; close enough that I might rip the throat out of any questions that sent her hastening back to her bedroom like a scorched cat.

'...wouldn't tell me what was happening.'

I caught the tail-end of my daughter's comment, and I could guess how it began. In the few days that had passed, Jess and I had spoken again of her worries that there had been something going on with Ryan, or in Ryan's life, that he wasn't willing to tell her. She said she'd imagined horrible things: other girls; plans to skip town; depression even. It couldn't hurt for her to share those worries with the people best placed to do something with them now. I didn't know what was useful to the police, but I was glad she was telling them the truth.

'And,' Shaw started, 'the night that Ryan was attacked. You say you were here?'

There was a long pause before my daughter said, 'Yes.'

'Is there anyone who can corroborate that?'

And just like that, my stomach was an ocean wave in a winter storm. *Why the fuck should anyone need to?* I wanted to say. *Look at the girl! Someone has killed her boyfriend and she's broken with grief and here you are–* But I swallowed it all and only stepped around the corner, meekly, like a woman not possessed and asked, 'Sorry, sugar with the teas, or…'

Jess erupted into a shoulder-shuddering-mess of tears. I didn't need to ask why: Ryan always took two with his tea.

CHAPTER EIGHT

If the grieving girl won't go to Muhammad, then the mountain has to come to our house for dinner. It was days after the police visit when I eventually gave up on the prospect of getting Jessica to go to Freya's house – which she saw as Ryan's house now, a walking tour of reminders for her broken heart to stare into. So instead, I invited Freya and Kaleb to ours. To begin with they didn't want to leave their tomb either; it was the one place, I suspected, where my beautiful friend could still feel close to her beautiful boy, where she might go upstairs at any point and inhale a memory of him, or sob into an old jumper that still held his scent. I'd found her with her head buried in the folds of his football hoodie earlier that day, after the phone call from the police. The preliminary medical examination had been done on Ryan's body, and we had all spent the afternoon sat quietly in our respective homes buried under the weight of knowing how he'd died.

There had been blunt force trauma to the head, before. Then, there was some kind of manual strangulation. There was guesswork already that the blow to the head may have subdued him for long enough for everything that came afterwards –

though I didn't know whether that was official guesswork, or Freya's mind running with the hideous details of it. 'Some fucking animal strangled my boy,' was how she told me, and though I'd held her and shushed her and tried to comfort her ill-ease, she was entirely right. I, too, found that when faced off with the news of how Ryan had died, I was thinking less of the death now, and more of the monster who had done it. Because of course, they had to be some kind of monster. When Theo died, I raged against anyone who may have had the smallest input into his death; including the car brand, and the developers who I repeatedly berated for not having done a better fucking job at reinforcing the steel shell of the vehicle. But to know there was some*one* responsible, to know there was one single person who'd engineered this loss– I tried to shake it away before it could take hold as I sliced through the centre of another full red pepper. And I tried to ignore the blood spurt it sent across the chopping board in my kitchen.

Jess and Kaleb were in my living room watching a comedy show that was, by the grace of God, stirring the occasional burst of laughter. It was a curt-sharp-harsh sound and I thought I caught Freya flinch whenever she heard it.

'I don't know how they're laughing,' she eventually said.

'Neither do I,' I admitted. 'But I'm glad that they are.'

A heavy sigh tumbled out of her. 'Bloody strangled, Ann.'

I dropped my knife then, and pulled her into a hug. 'They'll catch the bastard.'

'They'd better,' she said into my neck, 'because I don't know how I'll go on living if they don't.' She squeezed me hard, once, then pushed me away. 'Anyway, what are we even making here exactly?'

'Wait, I thought *you* knew,' I said, mustering the best jovial tone I could manage. It caused a smile to crack across her face but the frown that followed after made me worry that even that small flicker of amusement had physically hurt her. 'We're making a vegetable medley.'

'Which is what, exactly?'

'It's a medley.'

She waited a second before asking. 'Of vegetables?'

'See, you do know what we're making.'

She didn't laugh and I couldn't blame her. It was a worthless attempt at humour, and I didn't know why I was resting on the idea of making Freya laugh when in the days after Theo's death I'd hardly even spoken. The FLO had stressed the importance of keeping busy, though, and in private she'd suggested to me that we might find things that required active engagement, too: cooking; some visits out of the house, if anyone or everyone could manage it. But it was easier said than done, and I thought a woman who dealt with this for a living should know better than to suggest cooking a fucking meal might ease the grief of murder and– I exhaled slowly while I cut into a green pepper. I had been trying all damn day long to keep my own feelings in a small bottle; the type you might imagine tying a knot of rope around and throwing into the sea for posterity's sake. But now, knowing what had happened to Ryan – or at least, having the early ideas of it – everything felt that bit worse. And while Freya sobbed and Kaleb stared into space and Jessica stole glugs of wine when she thought I wasn't looking, I found that I could only manage anger.

I couldn't criticise Jess for the drinking, though it wasn't something I would encourage long-term either. Still, we'd always been a household of letting her try small amounts from a sort-of-young age, to try to demystify the attraction as she got older. But I'd realised at about lunchtime that the lemonade she was downing was also loaded with white wine, and there was a full bottle missing from the fridge. I imagined her having stashed it in her room somewhere; not that she was leaving her room for long enough periods for me to investigate that theory. This was the longest she'd been out of her den for, too, and I didn't want to rock that boat until it became necessary. When I heard another belch of laughter from the living room, though, an unmistakably drunken cackle, I wondered whether it was worth excusing myself to check now.

I set my knife down and wiped my hands clean on the front of my jeans. 'I'm just popping upstairs for a second.'

'She's had about two thirds of a bottle,' Freya answered without missing a beat. She was grating the skin off a carrot in sharp and livid movements. 'I checked the last time I went to the bathroom. It's in the bottom drawer, inside her wardrobe. It was wedged under a bag of old clothes.' A small sound fell out of her then, like a strangled cry she was trying to swallow back down. She turned to face me. 'I know a drunk teenager when I see one.'

I ran a hand through my hair and dropped into a seat at the table. 'Should I say something?'

'Not yet.' She turned and went back to grating. 'Let her have her ease.' Freya was so focused on her task that she didn't seem to notice that she'd whittled the carrot down to a sharp stake; now it looked like an implement that might take someone's eye out with the right force, or at least do some measurable damage. And I wondered whether she was thinking again of the person who had taken her son. *How can she be thinking of anything else?* I wondered as I heaved myself up from the seat and went back to the sideboard.

The kitchen was a mess of colour. There were explosions of vegetables everywhere: sweet potatoes; green beans; every shade of pepper. The meal was going to be impossibly large by the time we'd finished; enough to feed a family of five. Which of course, we no longer were.

'Is this even helping?' I asked, suddenly defeated by the whole endeavour.

Freya paused again, as though giving the question serious thought. 'Yes, I think it is.'

Another hour had rolled by when we called Kaleb and Jessica in to eat, the table set with cutlery, wine and candles, like it was a sophisticated occasion. At least I'd managed to make the distractor task look presentable. In the time it had taken for vegetables to roast and sausages to cook through and onion gravy to boil, Freya had cried three times and I had, indulgently, joined her for one of those outbursts. I was exhausted with trying to be strong for this, but whenever my resolve started to waver I thought of the long bath I would run later, the wine I would pour – assuming there was a drop left in the house – and the deep and shoulder-shuddering cry I would have in that privacy, and I henceforth vowed to hold myself in until then.

Jessica didn't manage the same holding pattern. She stepped into the kitchen clutching onto Kaleb's arm, and stared blankly at the four spaces laid on the table. The expression she wore was a confused one, as though she were seeing the formality of a family dinner for the first time in her life. Though of course, I knew that her muddle stemmed from the uncanniness of this family dinner in particular; the strange and absent place setting, the spectral elephant in the room. Her shoulders started to shudder-judder like tears were coming again and there was a collective intake of breath from the adults; the parent in us bracing for the hurt of a child. But instead of shielding her eyes, she covered her mouth, and the tremors continued.

'Mum, I think I'm going to–'

And with that she bolted from the room, up the stairs; her exit punctuated by the slam of the bathroom door above us.

There was a long pause before I spoke. 'I'm sorry.'

Kaleb closed the distance between us and pulled me into a hug. 'She's hurting, we all are.' Somewhere behind me he must have beckoned Freya to join, because I soon felt her own shaking arms wrapped around my back, reaching for her husband beyond me. When Kaleb broke the embrace up seconds later, he kissed my forehead and then leaned in to kiss Freya's cheek. 'We have to eat, right?'

'Do we?' she snapped, and I shot her a hooded look which she missed.

Kaleb pulled out a chair for himself. 'Frey, come on. You've cooked all this.'

'How can you eat, Kaleb? How can you fucking laugh?'

'Freya,' I warned, but from the glare she shot me then, I was worried she'd turn on me, too, if I pushed too hard. 'You need to eat something to keep your strength up.'

'I don't care about my strength, Annie.' She rubbed her palm over her face and revealed a theatre mask of tears when the hand was moved away. 'I'm going to check on Jessica. She might need... I don't know, something.'

Kaleb waited until she'd left the room before he spoke. 'I feel as though she hates me.'

I reached across the table to grab his hand. 'She hates everything at the minute, Kaleb. Everything about the whole world.'

Kaleb and I ate in near silence then, with the occasional scratch of cutlery on crockery, and dry-retching that was carried down from upstairs.

When we'd cleared up the crime scene of my kitchen, surfaces wiped clean of vegetable juices and half-eaten leftover food thrown in the waste disposal, I sat and watched an episode of the same comedy that he'd been watching with Jess earlier in the night. Neither of us laughed, though midway through the episode I stole a look in his direction and saw quiet tears rolling down his cheeks, just visible from the glow that the television screen threw on him. I reached across the sofa and grabbed his hand, and he squeezed back before pulling away from me.

When the credits for the episode rolled, he stood abruptly and announced he was going for a cigarette. He'd quit smoking on

Ryan's third birthday – cold turkey, as though it was nothing to give up a bad habit for the sake of staying around longer for his son, which he'd told me was his reason for it – but without that incentive, Kaleb had already fallen back on the crutch of it, and I wasn't about to criticise him. I told him I'd check on the girls while he was out.

There hadn't been any movement upstairs for the stretch of the episode we'd watched. So I crept quietly, in the hope that one or both of them might finally be managing to rest, in the company of each other's discomfort. When I reached the top of the stairs I could see there wasn't a light on in the bathroom, so I headed straight for Jessica's room instead. I eased the door open, one crying hinge at a time, and saw their outlines. They were curled together, Freya tucked around Jessica's sleeping form; Freya's own deep-sleep-breathing clear from the rise and fall of her shoulders. The two people I loved most in the world, and I couldn't do anything for either of them. So instead I only lingered in the doorway a while longer, as though I might protect them during their respite. But of course, there was nothing left for me to protect either of them from in those moments; the worst had already happened to them.

CHAPTER NINE

'I don't think this is a good idea,' I said as we pulled up to the school gates.

'I have to go back sometime.' Jessica was looking out of her window as she spoke, staring into the abyss of the football field that was still fenced off with police tape. They hadn't even cleared the area yet, and I didn't understand how Jess could face the sight of it every time she moved from the school buildings to home. But I didn't feel like I could question anything by then either. *Nothing about this is normal,* I reminded myself, often, whenever the abnormal faced me down. 'If it's too much then I'll come home.' She turned to me then. 'You called ahead and told–'

'The teachers know, sweetheart, of course,' I interrupted.

'They will have said something to my class. To the school, maybe.' She flashed a sad smile and nodded. 'They're all good people.'

Something about the sentiment felt too old to belong to her, and it was enough to nearly bring me to tears. *But I will not,* I cautioned myself, *I will wait until she is out of the car. I will wait until I am home.* Jessica climbed out without another word – not even a goodbye – and far from waiting until I was home, I was hardly out of the school gates when I found that I needed to steer over and throw my hazard warning lights on. The tears came thick and fast, and when I pulled my hands away from my hot face I saw they were streaked with the make-up that I'd put on only an hour earlier. I hadn't cared how I looked; I'd only been looking for something to keep my idle hands busy while Jess was getting ready. I felt my heart thrum with such a force then, that I thought I might have somehow swallowed it down into my gut and I tried, tried, tried in vain to get my breathing under control. I wound the window down and gulped in air like a creature recently emerged from water, and when the cool of the morning hit my face I was thankful for its sting.

I had watched Ryan grow up. I had been in the same room as him when he'd taken his first steps, swapping nervous looks with Freya who had puckered her lips and placed a finger in front of them to encourage quiet for the monumental occasion. I had been there when he boasted of *two* lost baby teeth; one of which he must have swallowed during the night, the only evidence of it then being the gaping space in the front of his mouth that had left him wide-smiled, with only his childish pride remaining. And I had seen him go from child to young man, when he came to collect my daughter for their end of school dance as they shifted from Junior to Senior. He had even asked my permission to ask her, even though they'd been courting each other for some time before it. I had been there; I had been there. And it was a physical burden that Ryan would never be *there* again. And though I tried to plug that wormhole of thinking, I found that nothing apart from more tears, deeper and more ragged breaths, more tears again – even though I had finally found energy enough to pull the car away from the kerb, too – would provide a temporary ease for the pain of it all. I tried to blink away feelings as I approached a junction but then–

The front of her car hit the front of mine.

'Were you even looking, you silly cow?' The voice was loud

and taut and angry – and it was the first real distraction I'd had in days.

The damage was superficial. The front of both cars were dented; mine worse than hers, which felt only right, karmically speaking. The woman, who had soon seen that I was tear-stained and shaking – not from the crash even, only from life – changed her tone then, took my details and went about driving her children to school. Meanwhile, I drove straight to Freya's. She wasn't due to be working, and when I arrived I found her outside the house again painting another coat of black over her front door. I couldn't work out whether it was a symbolic gesture or a desperate one; something to keep her hurt busy. She turned, paintbrush in hand, black tar dripping onto the paving slabs of her porch step, not that she seemed to mind. Her eyes widened and I realised she must have noticed the car.

'What the hell happened?'

'I had an argument with a Ford Focus.' I locked the vehicle and trod down to her, while she set the paintbrush to stand awkwardly in the pot. 'I thought you'd already covered the yellow.'

She shrugged. 'Kaleb has gone to work.'

'Jess has gone to school.'

Freya stepped forward and wrapped two arms tight around me. She spoke into the collar on my coat. 'Shall we drink tea all day and take it in turns to cry?'

I laughed; a sad huff of a noise. 'I came here to support you.'

'Then I hope you brought bloody good scaffolding.'

We went into the house then, and I saw that the front door wasn't the only thing Freya had started to tear her way through. The hallway – once patterned with a deep maroon wallpaper, polka dotted with a cream floral print – was stripped bare. There were rough ribbons of it all over the floor, leading to a stack of precariously balanced photo frames at the bottom of the stairs: Ryan's pictures, featuring Freya and Kaleb throughout the years. I said nothing of the state of the place until we got into the kitchen. But there, more chaos ensued. Every cupboard door was open and emptied of tins, bottles, jars, all of which were wedged around each other on the work surfaces.

'I couldn't sleep.' She was facing away from me, filling the kettle with water already. 'I knew there was herbal something or other lying around in one of the cupboards but could I find it?' She slammed the kettle back onto its stand and water spilled from the spout. 'Could I fuck. So I thought, do you know what I'm going to do? I'm going to–'

'Strip the wallpaper in the hallway?'

She turned and nearly, *nearly,* smiled, but it was an uncomfortable expression. 'After I emptied the cupboards, and didn't find the herbal drink, I decided I needed something else to keep busy with. There's so much leftover wallpaper in that spare room and I just thought, that will be a good project. Then I took all the pictures down, and…' She rubbed hard at her face and sighed. 'Then I decided that I would leave everything out, in here, so I could actually go through it all. How often do we go through our cupboards? We just stockpile shit.' She knocked at a jar of ready-made Bolognese sauce as though it had done something to offend her. 'I'll sort this out over the day. But the police are coming round later, I think. So, I don't know, I'd better do it before they get here.'

I tried to keep my tone neutral. 'Do you know what they're coming for?'

'Another non-update.'

It had been just over a week since Ryan. *Shouldn't they have found something by now?* I wondered, though I truly didn't know. My frame of reference for these things flowed from ITV docu-dramas and rubbish Netflix series that Jessica had once upon a time made me watch. Though I suspected any mention of true crime would be banned for life from our home after this.

'They're coming to ours this evening,' I offered instead.

Her head snapped up. 'Do *you* know why?'

'Something about a DNA sample from Jess. They said it's–'

'To rule out the samples they've found, the ones from…'

She didn't need to complete the sentence. They had already told me they were looking to make eliminations from samples taken from Ryan's clothes, hair, body. I hadn't told Jessica they were coming. I didn't want them to catch her by surprise, of course, but once she'd made the decision to shower, dress, leave the house without my cajoling her into it, the last thing she needed was to know there might be two detectives waiting for her at the end of the school day.

'Look,' I crossed the kitchen to her, 'I've got an idea.' I thought again of what the FLO had said. *Try to keep them busy,* I parroted back as I collected a packet of pasta sheets from the back of the worktop. 'You're going to sort through all of this anyway, and you said cooking the other night helped to keep you busy, so–'

'Annie, I don't want to think about eating.' She sounded exhausted, and I wondered whether Kaleb had also suggested a million things for Freya to keep busy with. Though from the state of the kitchen, the hallway, the front door, she was managing to keep busy with some things already.

'Okay.' Another bright idea. 'Then we can put all this stuff to good use anyway, you can cook, and you don't have to eat. How's that for a deal? We can make up a load of meals and take a drive out to the shelter in town, and we can just drop them there. That would be a good thing to do, wouldn't it?'

Freya turned away and grabbed the tea caddy. She made drinks silently and I didn't push any further until we were sitting at the table, each of us cradling a steaming mug.

'I'm sorry I can't take this away, Freya. I'm sorry I can't…'

There was a long pause before she said, 'I want to talk to Jessica.'

'Okay…' Jessica couldn't look her in the eye still. Whatever closeness Jess shared with Kaleb – while she was slamming down white wine like a teenager uncorked for the first time – she hadn't been able to emulate with Freya. She hadn't said as much, but I'd seen it. 'What about?'

'About Ryan, obviously. She knows more than anyone about his friends, where he was going, who he was involved with. This can't have been a senseless thing, Annie, it just can't. There must be a reason why someone, *someone*, went after him, and if the police can't bloody work it out then I sure as hell will.'

'Freya,' I tried to be gentle, 'it's such early days, sweetheart.'

She huffed; a frustrated and dismissive noise. 'You sound like Kaleb.'

Kaleb is right, though, I wanted to say, but didn't. Because how would that help anything? Instead, I reached across to grab her free hand; I nearly winced at the cold, and I wondered when she'd last eaten a proper meal. I gave two quick squeezes which caught her attention, and she looked up at me then, with eyes that were full of feeling and tears and tiredness.

'Freya, I *know* how hard this is and–'

She snatched her hand away and cut me off in the process. Something had turned in her, I saw, and the feeling was something less sad and more like maroon rage. 'How do you know exactly?' She stood and threw her tea into the sink, then slammed her mug on the sideboard as though punctuating a point she hadn't made yet. 'How could you possibly know what any of this is like, Annie? I can't get my boy back,' she stabbed at her chest with a pointed finger then turned it on me, 'meanwhile, *you*, you can go out and get yourself a new husband whenever you want!'

The comment cut right through me. I imagined that if I looked down, I might see a gaping hole in the centre of my chest where air was leaking out. But I decided to let her have that blow. In a morbid way, she was right. I couldn't know what I'd do if something were to take my girl. *Someone,* I corrected myself. Because of course, there was nothing accidental about losing Ryan. He'd been snatched away.

Freya looked at me like she was waiting for an argument then, but I didn't have one in me. If she needed blind fury, she would have to look elsewhere. 'I think I should go,' I said, and stood. When I turned for the door I saw Kaleb lingering there; his face a horrified picture. And I thought Freya would likely get the argument she needed after I'd gone.

CHAPTER TEN

Jessica was a child scorned. She sat on the sofa with her hands on her knees, and I wondered whether she was trying – but clearly failing – to keep her hands steady. The police had arrived in the early evening. And even though Jessica had been home since lunchtime – she'd stormed through the front door without an explanation, and following Freya's outburst, I hadn't had energy enough to put myself in the firing line – I hadn't forewarned her the detectives would be coming. DS Haynes asked her to open her mouth wide and Jess followed instructions, still child-like, as though opening for a doctor to inspect a sore throat. I half-expected Haynes to ask her to say, 'Aaah.' Or maybe Jessica would do it without prompting, as a knee-jerk reaction. After Haynes had swabbed her mouth, Jess closed it and resumed her stock position of staring at nothing at all on the floor in front of her; she looked stunned then, with a second wave of shock hitting her. *Or is it a fourteenth, twentieth, hundredth wave of shock by now?* I wondered. *Will the shock of this ever fade?* Haynes bagged the sample and then turned to catch my attention.

'Do you mind?'

'Oh, no,' I answered, 'of course not.' It hadn't crossed my mind that they would need my DNA, too, though I had no frame of reference for how thorough these eliminations would be.

'Why do you need hers?' Jessica asked then, and the sound of her voice stunned me. It came out in a croak, and I couldn't decide whether it was lack of use – from her afternoon of not speaking to me, that is – or whether it was influx of emotion.

'It's just protocol,' DC Shaw answered. 'It'll help, further down the line, if we have everything we need from the start.'

Haynes swabbed the inside of my cheek and then bagged this second sample. 'Thank you,' she turned, 'and thank you, Jessica. I know how difficult a time this is for everyone here, and these eliminations, well, they're not exactly pleasant.' She was packing everything away into a secure case as she spoke. 'We'll be in touch as and when there are developments. Thank you both again.' She moved to leave the room but Jessica pulled her back with another question.

'You still don't know what happened then?'

I thought I heard Haynes sigh. 'It's still very early days, Jessica. We're working hard to find out what happened to Ryan though, I can promise you that much.'

When Jess didn't answer I stepped in with a thank you instead, then I saw the detectives to the door. Haynes promised to be in touch if there were changes in the case, and gratitude poured out of me for a second time. I closed the front door and rested my head against the cool surface of it for a second, long enough for a deep inhale. My mouth was poised in a perfect circle to breathe out when, from somewhere behind me, Jess spoke.

'Did you know they were coming?'

I turned and recognised a similar expression to the one Freya had shown me earlier in the day. Ryan's death was making Furies of them both.

'They'd told me they were coming, yes, but–'

'Don't,' she interrupted me, 'just don't.'

She bolted back up to her room then and slammed the door hard enough to rattle the bones of the house. I decided to save any wasted time in making dinner, or even suggesting it, and instead I poured out a large glass of wine for myself. I sat, and drank, and listened to the dull thrum of Jessica's music upstairs. I don't know how much time rolled by.

The front doorbell was such a loud intrusion that I flinched when the noise hit me. I was at the bottom of the stairs, cheese sandwich in one hand and a packet of crisps in the other. Somewhere between my second and third glasses of wine, it had struck me that another bottle was missing. I couldn't tackle the conversation with Jessica. But the thought of her alone in her room, glugging wine straight from the bottle, drove me to throw together something, anything, to put some kind of lining in her stomach. I would knock and leave it outside, I decided; a peace offering, of sorts. But instead I wedged the crisps in the crook of my elbow and turned for the door; I was half-expecting Freya, or maybe hoping-praying-wishing for Freya. When I yanked the door open though, I found a woman I couldn't place. It took a second or two for the wine-watercolour image of her to clear well enough for me to realise where she belonged: Jessica's school. Her name escaped me entirely though, and I couldn't work out whether it was a cognitive lag from the alcohol or whether–

'Donna,' she said then, as though sensing my confusion, 'Morfett. I'm Bev Sykes' mum.' She smiled, then added, 'Divorced, maiden name.' It seemed an odd detail to add and I wondered how often she'd had to explain away the lack of a shared name with her daughter. 'I'm sorry, I've caught you at a busy time.'

I looked down at the sandwich. 'Oh.' I laughed. 'No, I… It's just a snack, for Jess. She's been struggling with food, since… Well, you know.' There was a long and uncomfortable pause then, before I managed to feign politeness. 'I'm so sorry, please,' I stepped aside, 'come in, come in. I'm just… I'll run this up to Jess's room, if you don't mind, and I'll be right with you. Is everything okay? With Bev?' I asked as she stepped into the hallway with me.

'I'm not sure.' An awkward noise fell out of her; it might have been a laugh, but I didn't know the woman well enough to guess. And the blurred edges of the situation – smudged still with white wine and too little food – made it difficult to read her expression. 'I'll just wait.'

'The living room is that way,' I gestured, 'take a seat, won't you? I'll only be a minute.' *Because my daughter won't talk to me anyway,* I held back from adding, though it stung me in the same way cheap red wine takes a layer from your throat. I headed for the stairs and trod gently to Jessica's room. The music had stopped. I knocked once, twice, without expecting a response and then set the food down outside the door. And I spoke in a low voice, to keep the sentiment hidden from the guest downstairs. 'I'm just setting something to eat down, sweetheart. Please, try?'

She might have answered; she most likely didn't. Though there was some comfort to be found in not knowing one way or the other. It was an easy lie to believe, that she might have found anything to say.

I hurried back downstairs to where Donna Morfett was sitting on the guest sofa, as though having an acute understanding for the layout of the room. She was surveying the space when I walked in. Her face was neutral, but the way she was playing around with a collection of bangles on her wrist made me think she was nervous. *Nervous because of what you have to say,* I wondered, *or nervous to be in a house so close to death?* When she spotted me in the doorway she smiled; she was wearing a light-red lipstick, and the rest of her face was painted in a soft porcelain which gave her something doll-like.

'Can I get you a drink?'

'I'm driving, but thank you.'

I thought it must speak to the stench of me that she'd assumed I could only offer booze.

'We have soft drinks, tea, coffee?' She shook her head then, so I only dropped onto the opposing sofa and asked, 'Sorry, Donna, what is it that I can help you with?'

When she spoke, she avoided eye contact. Her focus rested on my chin, or perhaps even my neck area, and I knew well enough that that alone could not be the sign of anything good. 'I don't know whether Jessica told you what happened at school today, between her and Bev?'

Jess isn't telling me anything anymore. 'No, she didn't mention. But look, Jess is going–'

'No, no,' she held her hands palm up to stop me, 'Jess didn't, hasn't, done anything wrong. That's not… That's not what this is about. Apparently, Bev was quite upset at school today, about the Ryan situation.' Involuntarily, I felt my head tilt; that seemed an interesting euphemism for the death of a classmate, on campus, in a suspected murder, too. I went off Donna for a second then, even though I knew the judgement was harsh. 'When Bev was upset, something got said about, oh, I don't know, she told Jessica that she had every right to be as upset about Ryan, or some such nonsense. I know,' she held up her hands for a second time, without my even moving to interrupt her, 'I *know* that was an unfair thing of Bev to say. But during this, this whatever it was that happened,' the further hesitation that came, then, made me brace with nerves, 'Bev told Jessica that Ryan was going to break up with her.'

My eyes widened, another unwilling gesture. But it felt as though someone had reached into the crack made from Freya's earlier remark and started to wrestle with the space there. 'Why would Bev say that?'

'I've tried to get to the bottom of it myself, Annie, but frankly,

Bev isn't telling me much more. She's obviously holding back on something. And I've told her it's a very serious business, and that if she knows something, anything, then far from playground gossip, it's actually something the police might need to know, too, and Christ,' she rested her elbow on the arm of the sofa and pressed her fingertips against her forehead, 'all that seems to have done is make her clam up even more. But I have been trying, over the evening, to get her to talk.'

Far from being interested in how willing Bev was to speak to her own mother, I more wondered whether she'd be willing to speak to the police. *Is this something the police* should *know?* I questioned. Though it was shortly followed by another, much more disturbing thought: *Was my daughter about to become a suspect here? Was this something that would become a motive?* I shook the idea away as an extreme one, fuelled only by too much wine and too many TV dramas.

'I don't really know what to do with this,' I admitted.

She flashed a sympathetic expression; a downturned smile. 'No, I'm not sure that I do either.' She managed to hold eye contact then, too, and I thought she must already feel better for having purged the information. 'I mostly came over here to apologise for it, because Bev, whatever she knows, she shouldn't have... Jess is going through enough, frankly, without a comment like that being made. Beyond that, I... I don't know what happens next. Do I report this?'

When the silence stretched out, I realised she was waiting for an answer. I thought back to what Freya had said, about wanting to speak to Jess about Ryan; who he spent time with, what he'd been doing. And it dawned on me that perhaps Jess wasn't the best person to speak to after all, considering what the rumour mill at school might know that she didn't. I tried to do fast maths and weigh up the right and wrong. As Jessica's mother, there was no easy answer. But if I were Bev's mother...

'I'll find the card for the detectives I've been dealing with. If Bev knows something, it's best that she talks to them.'

Donna nodded and dropped her eyes again. I wondered whether she'd been hoping that I would say something else. 'Thank you, Annie.'

After I handed over DS Haynes' details, there wasn't much else that either of us had left to say. Donna apologised, again, for what had happened, and how it had happened, and I wanted to console her. But in truth, I wasn't sure I had many more consolations left in me after the day I'd already had, and the hurt I'd already had flung at me. Instead, I only thanked her for coming and saw her to the front door. She asked me to give her love to Jessica and I promised to, even though I already knew I wouldn't. In fact, if Jess hadn't heard the doorbell, I wouldn't acknowledge this visit at all. I made a point to close the door quietly when Donna left, in the hope that I could hide any damning evidence too. But I needn't have worried; Jess had greater distractions.

When I climbed the stairs to try to overhear signs of life – and to check whether the sandwich had gone – all I could gather was the sound of retching-gagging-sickness, and after a few seconds, the flush of the toilet.

CHAPTER ELEVEN

Kaleb texted me early the morning after the fight before. He didn't mention Freya, or what she'd said; instead, he only asked me to meet him: *Coffee? 11:30 @ Indie CoffCo?* I took it to mean that Freya wouldn't be coming. I texted back – *See you there* – and took my time in getting ready. I hadn't heard Jessica leave for school, and I guessed that must mean that whatever had passed between her and Beverley Sykes the day before had been enough to put her off. So on my way to the bathroom I gently tapped on her door, and opened it without waiting for a reply. At some time during the early hours of the morning, I'd decided that whatever she was thinking, feeling, she needed to know she wasn't alone – whether she wanted to be or not. She was sitting up in bed when I walked in, doing nothing but staring out of her open window. There was a horrible chill in the room.

When she turned I could see the tiredness in her; too tired, it seemed, to ignore me, or tell me to leave, because instead she broke the quiet before I even had the chance to. 'I'm sorry about all the wine.' Her voice was rough around the edges and I thought back to the sound of her retching the night before; the way the smell of vomit had lingered in our shared bathroom. She opened her mouth as though to speak again but her bottom lip only bobbed up and down, two, three times, and then her face crumpled into tears. 'I'm so sorry, Mum.'

And I rushed to her. I cradled her how I must have done a hundred times or more, from childhood through to this, and I let her sob hard against my shoulder until the damp soaked into my skin. 'Sweetheart, you have *nothing* to be sorry for,' I reassured her, though it seemed to make the tears come faster. 'This is horrible, Jessie, all of it just so horrible and I... I wish I could take it away, sweet girl.' I kissed the crown of her head and held her to me, as though if I could only hug her tight enough, I might force all of the tears out at once. Though of course, there would be tears over this forever, I knew, and that wounded me too. What kind of mother can live with knowing their child is forever hurt by something? Something they can't fix or take away or even soothe? 'I wish there was something I could do,' I said eventually, though I knew it was a feeble offering.

'You're doing loads,' she managed, her juddering tears slowing to a near stop. 'You're doing loads and I'm just being a bitch and–'

'You dare,' I pushed her away so I could get a view of her face, 'you dare call yourself that. You're doing the best you can in a horrible, *awful*, situation, sweetheart. Someone your age, Christ, someone *any* age, shouldn't be going through this.' Then I clutched her back close. 'But I'm here for you, okay? I'm always here for you, and you can always talk to me and cry and, Jesus, be angry, even.' I thought, then, of Freya, and the anger she'd shown me the day before. And I decided that after I'd seen Kaleb, and got a read of the situation at their home, I would call her. I would call and I would be a sponge to whatever she needed to throw at me because– 'When you love someone, you're always there for them. And I know that's how you felt about Ryan, and that, sweetheart, that's how I feel tenfold, okay? You're a young woman but you're my baby, too.'

Somehow my sentiment had cracked the dam and she cried

more then. Anything she said was inaudible, but I was beyond the point of needing her to explain anything. I felt it all pour out, soak through my T-shirt, spread across my skin. I would have taken all the feeling from her if I could.

The coffee shop was an assault on the senses in comparison to the quiet of home. Before I'd left, I'd gone into Jessica's room and tucked her duvet in around her, then set a soft kiss on her forehead; another childhood routine, though I'd resisted the urge of a bedtime story, or a prayer, like Theo might have done with her once upon a time. The shop was made up of tables for two and standalone booths set to house as many as six people. It was a working day though, so rather than friends socialising the place was instead populated by suits and ties hosting interviews, business exchanges, or otherwise escaping their offices for a while. I'd arrived with wet hair, scraped into a high bun, joggers and an old jumper. I was desperately out of place. But so was Kaleb, who I eventually found huddled into a corner booth, also wearing his own scruffy clothes from home. *So you didn't make it to work today either,* I thought as he stood to greet me. He wrapped his arms around me tight and planted a kiss on my cheek as I pulled away.

'You look how I feel,' I said, and I was thankful when he laughed. 'Do you want anything?' I gestured to the counter behind me.

'Oh, I told them I was waiting for someone. They're going to bring teas over now you're here. Did you want breakfast tea, or fruit?'

It was a trick question. Kaleb, the dentist, would never order a fruit tea; in much the same way as he would never put sugar in a breakfast tea. 'Nice try, but I know the answer to that riddle already.' It was a long-standing joke with us both; so old now, I couldn't even remember how it had started. 'Tea is perfect, though, thank you. I haven't had one today,' I said, as I sat opposite him and dumped my bag down beside me.

When I was settled, Kaleb stretched his arms across the table and held his hands palm up for me to hold. I took the cue. 'I cannot apologise enough for what Freya said yesterday.' I opened my mouth to push away the amends but he pressed on. 'Don't say it's okay, Annie, because it wasn't and we both know it. Grief is ugly, and she's going through it, but Christ, she isn't the only one who's lost Ryan.' I thought I heard a pang of frustration.

I clasped his hands and smiled. 'Thank you.'

'You're welcome.'

'But you still don't need to apologise,' I added.

'No, you're right; Freya does. But we all know that unless the Devil's planning to redecorate hell as an ice cave, you're unlikely to get an apology from her.' He leaned back then, and I soon saw why when a waitress lowered down a tray onto the table. She unloaded two pots of tea, along with two milk jugs, mugs and spoons, then disappeared quickly with a smile. 'Thank you,' Kaleb chased after her.

'Are you managing any sleep?' I asked as he collected together his tea: pouring, adding one splash of milk, then another. 'You look exhausted.'

He huffed a laugh. 'Did anyone ever tell you that you pay compliments wrong?' I reciprocated with a smile and a shrug. 'I'm getting a few hours, here and there. It's enforced rest, I guess. Freya and I, we both seem to be sleeping whenever and wherever we crash. It's hard, always waiting for a call, always waiting for… something.' I got the sense that perhaps he didn't know what they were waiting for, which made sense to me too. There was a lingering unknowing in all of this; a winter mist that hovered over the whole situation, stopping any one of us from seeing to the other side of Ryan's death. 'How are you doing? How's Jess?'

'Jess is drinking,' I blurted out.

'Annie, when we were there the other night–'

'She was drinking then, but she's been drinking since.' I ran a hand through my hair and then rested both elbows on the table. 'There are bottles of wine going missing. I've heard her upchucking three, four times, maybe. I know it's how she's handling it but… it doesn't feel much like handling it. She's a kid, you know? She shouldn't be drinking her way through her problems.' I sighed, then added, 'That's something she should do when she's our age.' I needed the gentle humour, to soften the blow of my outpouring. But I had to admit that it felt good to talk to another adult about Jessica too.

'Have you talked to her about it?'

'The drinking? No. But we talked like adults, and about Ryan, for the first time in days this morning and that felt like a monumental breakthrough.' I thought I saw Kaleb flinch at his son's name. 'I'm sorry, I…'

'No, no,' he was quick to jump in, 'there's nothing to apologise for. We should be talking about him. Christ, I think everyone in the whole world should be talking about him, about what happened. Maybe then we'd get some fucking results.' There were tears in his eyes, the further he trod into his sentences. 'I can't believe this is happening to us, Annie. I just can't.'

'Go on, you've had my outpouring. Let it out, Kaleb, let the whole lot out.'

'I'll cry,' he answered flatly.

'Then I'll get tissues.'

He held eye contact with me then, for a second longer than I expected him to. In that time, something shifted between us and I felt as though Kaleb was weighing me up for something. It was a full pause, packed with something he wanted to say. But then he snatched his stare away again and focused instead on bringing his mug to his lips and taking two deep gulps of the drink.

'What?'

'Can I talk to you in confidence?' he answered, and I felt my stomach shift over. Kaleb and I had known each other for as long as I'd known Freya, of course. And although Freya and I had always been closer – bonding over sore breasts in the beginning, all the way through to what we thought was the incoming of empty nest when the kids eventually left for university – Kaleb was a friend, too, and I wanted him to know that he had someone who he could turn to. But something about his tone made me fidget awkwardly in my seat, moving side to side like a child desperate for the bathroom. I had to answer honestly, though, and of course the answer was–

'You know you can.'

He pulled in a greedy breath and spoke into the table. 'My alibi for the night Ryan was killed isn't going to hold up.'

A swarm of bees settled around me like a neck brace. All I could hear was an angry-static-hum and I found myself physically shaking it away; I had to, before I could answer. Even then, though, I only managed to say, 'I'm sorry?'

'I said, my alibi isn't–'

'I heard what you said,' I snapped. The bees were still there, a dull drone in the background of my thinking, and it crossed my mind this might be what it was like to have tinnitus. How irritating, how utterly distracting, to live with a constant interference and–

'Annie?'

I looked up at Kaleb then, and I wondered how long I'd been quiet. 'I– I don't understand. Where were you? Freya said you were at some dental thing.'

'I was, for the first part of the night.' He paused, sipped. 'The police spoke to some colleagues who were there, and their story didn't match mine. I'd told the police,' he paused and took another sip of his drink, and I thought the confessional must be drying out his nervous mouth, 'I'd told the police I left at a certain time, but when they checked, one or two colleagues said

I'd left earlier. When the police spoke to me for a second time, I had to tell them.'

I waited for the end of the explanation, because of course there must have been one. But still, he took some prompting. 'You had to tell them what, exactly?'

He looked over my shoulder before he spoke and I guessed he might be making sure the coast was clear; that there weren't any wagging ears about to catch him out. 'I've been seeing someone else, Annie. I have been for–'

'I don't want to know,' I said, stopping him, my hands palm up as though to create a barrier between me and his words. 'Do you love her? Whoever she is.'

'Yes.' He avoided eye contact. I was glad he at least had the decency to look ashamed by the admission. 'But I'm not *in* love with her.'

'And are you *in* love with Freya?' I heard my tone; judgemental, fierce, protective. I was ready to rip the innards out of the man who was shitting on my best friend. But when that man is also a friend, what do you do? Do you only leave a scratch instead, or do you still go for the jugular?

'I've been in love with Freya from about five minutes into meeting her.'

It felt like a bullshit response, and it wasn't going to soften me, if that's what he'd been hoping. If he loved Freya that much, he wouldn't have been seeing someone else. At least Theo had the decency to only have a one-night stand; a slip, he called it, and my response had been less than savoury – although entirely justified. But it made it that bit easier to believe he and I had something worth saving. If it had been a full-blown affair, I wasn't so sure things would have gone the same way.

'Then you need to tell her.'

'It'll ruin my marriage.'

'I don't imagine it'll save your marriage if the police tell her first.'

'They might not.' He looked desperate then, desperate and in need of comfort. 'Right? There genuinely might not be a need.'

But I couldn't give him what he was after. I thought hard for a second, waded through the lingering buzz to come away with stings on my hands, to find what felt like a right answer. 'Well if you don't, and they don't, then I will.' I pushed my tea away and collected my bag from the seat. 'So you have to play the odds.'

I may not go for the jugular. But I wasn't about to comfort the cheating shit either.

CHAPTER TWELVE

In the hours after I saw Kaleb, I paced so fervently in front of the window of our living room – in case Freya were to come steaming down the road, a woman in need, and I could have wine and tissues and a cleaver ready – with my phone clutched in hand, too. Kaleb aside, though, I wasn't prepared to go a full day without speaking to her. I hadn't, not since Ryan, and today wasn't going to be the day either, regardless of how she and I had left things. In the end, I managed to wait myself out until the sun started to dip and when the room sank into an orange hue I eventually hit dial. She answered after two rings.

'I'm sorry.'

I paused and looked out of the window, in case the world outside were suddenly a scene of crystals and ice. This was a living hell we were all trapped in, surely, but it didn't look to have frozen over, how Kaleb predicted it might if Freya were ever to muster an apology.

'It doesn't matter.'

'It does matter, Annie, you're… you're being so good, and I love you, and I… I'm fucking angry, with the world, but I sure as shit shouldn't be taking that out on one of the few people who are trying to help me. So, I'm sorry.' I glanced outside again, in case that second apology sealed it, but everything still looked the same. 'Are you okay?' she asked, then, 'Are you coming over?'

I sank into the sofa. 'Is Kaleb there?'

'No,' she sounded hesitant, 'he's popped out to get some bits. The police have been over and… there was news, some news. Christ, I don't know what counts as news. Annie, I want to ask something but please don't be offended?'

My stomach clenched. As a prefix, it didn't help me to feel especially calm about whatever was coming. 'Okay, what's happening?'

'Is Jess– Has Jess ever– Jessica, she isn't doing drugs, is she?'

'Wait, what?'

'Jess, drugs. Annie, I'm sorry, I know it's a horrible question, and it isn't, it absolutely *isn't* an accusation, but is she, do you think? Or even, has she ever, or…'

I felt my bottom lip bob up and down twice; I was dumbstruck. Of all the things I had braced for in this conversation, this topic hadn't even made a top ten of possibilities. Of course my daughter isn't doing drugs, I wanted to say, what an utterly ridiculous thing to ask. But of course, *every* parent wants to say that of their child, don't they? Every parent wants to eagerly dismiss the mere suggestion of foul behaviour, always. But I knew already that if Freya was asking this, she was asking for a reason – and I knew the reason had to be related to Ryan too.

'She's never done drugs, Freya,' I answered plainly, 'not that I'm aware of.'

I heard a sigh fall through the speaker. 'The police are trying to make me believe Ryan was. Doing drugs, I mean.' There came a long pause, and I thought I was meant to fill the space, but I was too busy picking apart her sentence. *The police are trying to make me believe*, as though there was something conspiratorial in it all. 'They found drugs in his system,' she blurted out then, and I realised that the police weren't trying to convince her of anything; they were just giving her the facts as they knew them. *But you wouldn't want to believe it either,* I reminded myself, *if this were Jess, you wouldn't want to think it.* I didn't want to think it of her *now,* but having heard this discovery from Freya, I found I was already second-guessing the resolve I'd had only minutes ago when I answered her question.

Jessica is a good kid, I cautioned myself, *don't think this of her...* Which was a fine argument bar one thing: Ryan had been a good kid too.

'Freya, I...' I started but gave up before an ill-fitting sentence could form.

'I know. I know. I can't get my bloody head around it either.'

'Have they said what?' I don't know why I asked; it might have been to fill the space forming in the phone call, or it might have been morbid curiosity. *Or it might be so you know what to look out for...*

'They gave some fancy names for things that I didn't understand. Kaleb nodded like he knew but he doesn't have a bloody clue either. We're not these people, Ann, you know? We're not the parents who have drugs in the house, whose kid can have drugs in the house...' She sounded defeated and I wanted to hug her. 'They're talking to others from the party, from the night... Jessica, she wasn't there, was she?'

'No, I assumed she would be with Ryan and all. But she was here all night.'

'Do you know why?'

Because she sensed Ryan was about to break her heart? I wondered, looking up to the ceiling, the other side of which lay my resting daughter and her heart that had somehow ended up broken all the same. 'I honestly don't, no. She hasn't even mentioned it, Freya, honestly. She said once during a crying fit that she should have been there, but I don't know whether that means she was meant to be going or–'

'She should have been there.'

'She should have been there,' I echoed. A sadness elbowed its way into the call then, and stuck itself out at awkward angles. It was a burden Jessica was going to carry for the longest time, and I hated that already. 'Freya, can I ask you something now?'

'Anything.'

'Ryan,' I said his name softly, as though trying not to crack an egg, 'had he said anything to you about, maybe, being unhappy with Jessica?'

She went quiet for a second, and I imagined her thinking. 'Genuinely not a word. The last time I asked about them, which was a little while ago, I'll admit, he did that dopey grin. You know the one he used to do when...' Her voice broke and a thick yolk of feeling dripped out. *When he was happy,* I autocompleted the sentence for her, because of course I knew exactly the face she meant. 'Why do you ask?'

I lingered for a second over whether to be honest. 'There are some rumours going around the school. Some girl, Bev someone or other. She told Jessica that Ryan was going to break up with her.'

'Bev Sykes?'

'You know her?'

'I know her mother.' Freya's tone was flat. It didn't seem important to push, but I was curious what run-ins she might have had with the girl's mother to give such a frosty response. 'Tell Jess to pay no mind to it, Annie, honestly. Kids are... they're fucking spiteful. It'll be something of nothing. Ryan...' Again, the same slow drip release of feeling came with his name. 'He loved her.'

From Freya's kindness, I wanted to offer something in return. But I wasn't sure whether it was like for like, exactly. I couldn't give her anything that wasn't going to hurt. But still, it felt important to own up to knowing. 'Do you know that Ryan was missing school? Skipping school, I mean.'

She huffed. 'A lot of school, I hear.'

So someone had beat me to it...

'Honestly, Annie, who the hell was my son?'

I couldn't imagine how lost she must feel. Her voice came to me through a woodland of confusion and a horrible part of me already thought that, somehow, there would be more trees to axe down before anything like an answer became clear. But if these early answers were anything to go by, I couldn't see future ones being anything that would ease the grief – more like pour gasoline over it instead, only for someone to strike a match and walk away.

'I'll ask Jess,' I said then, because I felt a desperate need to give her something; to rub aloe vera on the burn of all this. 'I'll talk to Jess and see if she knows anything about drugs going around the school.'

'I'm in here,' Freya said, and it took a second for me to register she wasn't talking to me. 'I'm on with Annie.'

In the background I heard Kaleb ask, 'Is she coming over?'

'No,' Freya answered for me, 'she's going to stay home tonight, with Jess. They're going to talk. Is that right, Ann? You'll do it tonight?'

I took the nudge. 'Of course, tonight.'

There was a stilted goodbye between the three of us then. I told Freya I loved her, and I was a call away. I asked her to give my best to Kaleb; deliberately loose, I didn't know what 'best' I was passing along to him anymore. Best insult, best right hook, best, 'You bastard, how dare you?' Freya said she'd ring if there was any more news and I promised the same.

When the call disconnected, I only sat for a moment and watched the outside world, dimming into angles shaped by streetlights and cars making their way home. I dropped my mobile on the window ledge and ran two hands through my hair, cradling the back of my skull as though the weight were too heavy now for my neck alone. That's how everything was beginning to feel: too heavy. And not for the first time, I tried to pull together the memory of Theo's voice; consider his gentle kiss to the forehead; and his commendable ability to say a terrible joke at exactly the right time. *But of course, there isn't anything funny to find here, is there?* I thought as another car rounded into our street.

I flicked on a light and made for the doorway. I had promised Jessica I wouldn't push too much with a hearty dinner, but that didn't mean I couldn't at least try another small meal. By the time she came through this, I imagined her having lived entirely on cheese sandwiches and ready salted crisps for as long as it took to find Ryan's killer. *Ryan's killer*. The words rolled around like a marble lost in a pinball machine and I gulped a deep swallow to settle what felt like bile in my throat.

Two steps out the door of the living room and I came to a dead stop. Jessica was there, crouched in the stairs with her chin resting against her knees. She wasn't a seventeen-year-old anymore; instead, I saw her as I'd seen her too many times as a child, hovering, listening into whatever Freya and I were saying. That part was no different, at least; she must have heard me on the phone.

When she looked up at last, I saw her eyes were red around the edges. She looked as though she hadn't slept properly for days; she most likely hadn't. And I toyed with the idea of offering her one of my old sleeping pills – only one – but it didn't seem right or safe given what I was about to ask either.

I opened my mouth to launch the question but she beat me to the punch.

'I wasn't doing drugs with him.'

I sighed. 'So you knew he was doing them?'

Her chin sank back to her knees. 'He'd started, a few months ago, I guess? It was one of the things that was different about him. I told him I didn't like it.' I felt a deep swell of pride in my girl then, but it somehow didn't feel right. 'He said it was a normal teenager thing to be doing. Told me I was boring, even, for not wanting to. I... I told him not to be a dick about it. At the time.' Her voice was flat and it struck me that her energy really must have dwindled to nothing by now. 'It was just weed to start with. I think he did stronger stuff now and then, when there was a party. But I don't know what, Mum, so I can't... I can't tell Freya.'

I sank onto the step two down from her. 'Why didn't you tell me, sweetheart?' *Or the police,* I thought, *should she have?* 'I could have spoken to Freya about it, or Ryan even.'

She shrugged. 'He already thought I was boring. Imagine if...'

I didn't need to imagine. Despite what my teenager thought, I'd been a teenager once, too, and I could remember the forceful cruelty of it. The taunts and accusations that stung like hornets might. She would see it as nothing, one day, but for a teenager in love I remembered all too well that there was nothing worse than being thought of as the boring one.

'Sweetheart,' I spoke quietly, as though that might soften the blow of the question, 'do you know where he was getting the drugs from? Was it someone at school, or...'

I knew the importance of dead air in a conversation like this. So I only waited, and rubbed the palm of my hand over the ball of her knee in what I hoped was soft support. Eventually she said, 'Connor. Connor Tolken. He's in our year.'

Later, when she was fed on half a cheese sandwich and two digestive biscuits, I trod back into the cold of my living room to find my phone. There was nothing from Freya, which might mean Kaleb still hadn't told her. Though of course, it could also mean that he had, and she was busy dismantling the house around them with a shouting match. Either way, I pulled up a fresh text and wrote only: *Drugs. Connor Tolken. Same year group.* And hit send.

CHAPTER THIRTEEN

Freya looked like a woman possessed. Her hair, while scraped back into a wild bun, was sticking out at science-fiction angles. There were pockets of bruising forming beneath each eye, too, that showed her lack of sleep. Her skin had somehow paled even more so in the three days that had passed – between Jessica giving us Connor's name, and Connor's mother agreeing to us coming over to the house to speak to him. I argued this as a job for the police, that we should pass the name along. But Freya had her own questions – and very little faith in the police, it seemed, that they would be asking the right things. I reassured her, over and again, that they knew what they were doing, but she looked to have little faith in that either. It was a grey and frostbitten Friday morning, and I could only imagine that all parents involved in this had places they'd rather be. Freya banged on the front door with a fist two times and she was moving for a third when I stopped her, setting my hand on her wrist, and instead I reached for the doorbell. She huffed at me like a teenager might. I wondered, not for the first time, why I had been called on for this job rather than Kaleb. Was it because he'd told her? While an affair might fade in comparison to the loss both of them were living through, I tried to reason whether it was something Freya would mention to me – or whether she really was too far gone in grief to care. The possibilities batted themselves back and forth in my mind like rowdy toddlers, and I soon came to think of it as a distractor task. While we were waiting for the front door to fall open – for what felt like an uncomfortably long time – I wrestled with whether he'd told her, whether she'd kicked him out, whether her big reveal, to me, was coming. Or whether the gas canister hadn't opened yet, and it was a blow that Freya still had to live through.

She bounced on the balls of her feet next to me and I reached down to squeeze her hand. 'Kaleb didn't want to come?' I asked, unable to keep the question in.

Another huff fell out of her, this time with an accompanying noise. 'He doesn't approve. Said something about waiting for the police to investigate things properly.' He had a point, I thought, but on principle I couldn't agree with anything that came out of his mouth now. *Funny how a friendship can shatter so quickly*, I thought, not for the first time since he'd admitted the affair. 'He won't be so quick to dismiss it when we find out what this little shit had given our son.'

I squeezed her hand again, then, as the door opened. Behind it there stood another equally exhausted-looking woman, and I worried that something might be sweeping through the neighbourhood in the wake of Ryan's death. Were we all about to find out things about our children that we'd rather not know? The thought gripped me in the guts, but I tried to smile all the same. Freya's face was set hard like rough concrete, and one of us needed to be approachable enough for this woman to talk to. Izzy Tolken was a small woman, in height and frame, and she stepped back without a word to welcome us into her home. Freya silently took the cue while I mustered a 'Thank you' for the both of us.

'Connor and Elliot are in the kitchen, if you follow the

corridor right down,' she said from behind us as she closed the door. 'I made a pot of tea… I wasn't sure, you know, if you'd want anything.'

'Thank you,' I said again; and again, Freya offered the woman nothing.

Jessica had said I'd probably recognise Connor when I saw him, but I didn't. Before meeting him that day, I wouldn't have been able to pick him out of a line-up. He was the average seventeen-year-old boy with too much gel in his hair and too many hormones for his face to know what to do with – and he looked terrified. Understandably so if the expressions of his parents were anything to go by. His father, a stocky man who also relied on too much hair product, slammed a hand on Connor's shoulder as he stood to greet us. I wondered what Connor would have done, if he'd been allowed to complete the gesture; would he have fallen at Freya's feet and begged forgiveness? Offered his hand and introduced himself as the boy who had sold drugs to her son?

'Please, take a seat,' Elliot said, while Izzy was already busy pouring tea for everyone as though running on automatic hostess mode. 'Freya, we want you to know that we've had strict words with Connor about all this business, and frankly, we're as outraged as you are.' He paused then, and locked eyes with his wife; he'd clearly realised the error. There was no one in the world who could be quite as outraged as the mother of the dead boy – though as his godmother, I felt sure that if there were a queue forming, the Tolkens still couldn't possibly be near the front when it came to hard-edged fury. 'I'm sorry, that was…' He shook his head, then started again. 'What I mean to say is we're obviously very disappointed with Connor, and I speak for Izzy as well when I say he'll be doing anything he can, and telling you anything he can, to help find out what happened to Ryan. Isn't that right?' He nudged his son, who stared at the table but nodded in agreement.

'I'm sorry,' he muttered.

'I can't do anything with sorry,' Freya answered, her tone flat. 'Do you mind if we get straight into this?' She took a seat at the table and I dropped in the chair next to her. 'I don't need too many details.'

On the drive over we'd tried to pool ideas together on what details she did actually want. Largely, we'd drawn a blank. Beyond wanting to know what Ryan was taking and how long he'd been taking it for; the why of the matter was something neither of us expected Connor to know. But it wasn't going to stop Freya from asking.

'Weed, mostly,' Connor said when Freya quizzed him about what Ryan was buying from him. 'There was this one time... there were pills.' He shook his head. 'Ryan didn't like it, though, he said something about them making him feel too out of control or... I don't know, something about it being like being drunk, but a bad version of it. He tried other things after that but...' The kid hesitated before he admitted, 'He wasn't only buying from me.'

'Fuck me,' Freya whispered, but in the cold quiet of the room it was loud enough for anyone to hear. I squeezed her knee beneath the table and then felt around for her hand.

'Jessica...'

My head snapped up at the sound of her name. 'Jessica what?'

'She never did anything. Or if she did, she wasn't getting it from me.'

'That doesn't get you points, Connor, if that's what you're thinking,' his mother snapped.

'How often was Ryan buying from you?' I asked.

The boy shrugged. He looked every bit the boy then: scolded, ashamed, caught taking more than his allowance's worth from the proverbial cookie jar. 'Every few weeks? There were times when he'd come back a bit sooner, I guess, but there were times when he bought more too.'

'Was he smoking it alone?' Freya pushed. 'Were there others involved?'

'It's a bit of weed,' he said then, in a sudden swap from shame to defensiveness. 'Most of the kids at school are doing it.'

'We don't care what the kids at school are doing,' Elliot said, his voice firm, and I spotted his son flinch at the sound. 'We care what you were doing, and what Ryan was doing. You stick to that, kid.'

'I'm sorry.'

'Does anyone at school know about this, Connor?' Freya asked, turning the topic back to something more relevant. 'Teachers, anyone?'

I caught a look pass between Elliot and Izzy when Connor answered, 'I told Mrs Day about it, after Ryan. I didn't know who else to go to and…' He petered out and glanced sideways at his father before he continued. 'I didn't know who else to go to, and I didn't know what I needed to be doing.'

Freya looked clueless, though, so I stepped in to ask, 'Sorry, Mrs Day the school counsellor? She knows about this?'

He nodded. 'She's the one who told Mum and Dad what had been happening. She said she wouldn't but–'

'Duty of care,' his mother interrupted him and I felt Freya tense next to me.

'It's a shame their duty of care hasn't extended to a phone call to me, isn't it?' She stood, and pushed her chair back in the process. It created an uncomfortable grind along the floor tiles; a wood-on-shine squeak followed as she kicked it further out of her way. 'You should be ashamed of that kid of yours,' she spat then, and turned for the door.

I flashed a tight smile to Izzy, then to Elliot, before I stood and followed after Freya. No one could blame her for the rage that was simmering to a boil; it was a wonder there weren't explosions everywhere she went at the moment, and she would have been entitled. I followed her out into the hallway and Izzy soon rushed out behind us.

'Are you going to the police?' she asked, her voice suddenly frayed around the edges. Freya made a sharp turn and pushed past me to get to the woman. 'I'm sorry, Freya, I… I know it's a horrible thing to have to ask, but of course we have to ask.' She looked from Freya to me and back again. 'Will you? Will you be going to them?'

'I'm more fucking stunned by the fact *you* haven't gone to them,' she answered and I braced myself. Freya wasn't a violent woman, but I was ready to dive in front of her then. There were only so many allowances that could be made for her, and I wagered that physical outbursts were a line in the sand for anyone. Even so, it was an inflammatory question if ever there was one. 'That little shit in there,' she pointed back into the room we'd just left, 'he deserves a punishment for what he's doing. How you haven't contacted them, how the *school* haven't contacted them, it's beyond me, it really bloody is.'

'Freya,' Izzy started, but Freya cut her off with a look.

'We will be going to the police, yes. Because my son was on drugs the night he died. Drugs that *your* son most likely sold him. And if that isn't something they deserve to know, Christ…' More followed, but it became inaudible as Freya yanked the front door open and paced out of the house.

'Izzy, I do understand,' I said then, speaking in a softer tone. And in many ways I did. It was another round of unwanted discoveries that involved more than just Ryan, and she was protective of her son in the same way Freya was of her own. 'But a boy is dead,' I reiterated, and I left the comment to hang. In part, I wanted to remind her; but in part, I needed to pause after the announcement, too, because the reminder was a brittle one to say aloud. I opened my mouth to add more, in the hope that emulating speech might trigger something, might help me know what to say, but I could only manage a headshake. 'Thanks for letting us talk to Connor. I realise it's difficult, but it's important too.' She moved to speak and I held up a hand to stop her. 'I'm not sure there's anything more that needs adding.'

I walked the driveway distance back to Freya, who was already in the driver's seat waiting for me.

'Get out,' I said as I pulled open her door.

'It's my car.'

'And you're not driving it in this state. Freya, get out.' I could see her hands shaking as she tried to key something into her phone. 'I'll drive you wherever you want to go, but I'm not having you drive this car.'

'Fuck's sake, Annie.'

I ignored her and took the keys as she climbed free of the vehicle. Once we'd swapped places I waited for her to buckle in before I geared the car up and pulled away from the house. I noticed then, that Izzy and Elliot were huddled together in the doorway watching us leave. They must have felt a deep dread in their bellies, and I nearly felt sympathy for them – nearly.

'Where are we going?' I asked as we neared the junction to their road.

'The school.' She pressed her phone to her ear. 'Hello… I'd like to make an appointment with Mrs Day… For now… Ten minutes from now will do…' I kept quiet while she made the call and I imagined a frantic secretary on the other end of the line; shuffling papers, making panicked gestures at anyone who happened to be close by. 'I'm coming in whether you can make an appointment or not… Well, quite, it's that very same duty of care that I've got some questions about… So you know who it is then, without me even saying, you know… You just tell her we'll be seeing her shortly.' She pulled the phone away then and stabbed the button to end the call. 'Snooty bitch. Duty of care, my arse. It's funny how everyone cares about that duty of care *now*, isn't it? But they didn't, Annie.' Feeling lodged in her throat and I could hear the prelude to tears. 'They didn't care when it was my boy.'

I indicated, pulled over and hit the hazard warning lights. 'We'll make them care, Freya.' She leaned towards me and I wrapped her in the tightest hug I could manage at the awkward angle. Her head rested in the crook between my shoulder and neck, her body tensed, and her tears poured out. And all I could hear on a winding loop, then, was that we needed to make them care; we needed to make *someone* care.

CHAPTER FOURTEEN

The room around us was so uncomfortably beige. I couldn't imagine how any student might come here to spill their innards, or worse still, ask for advice. Mrs Day had, conveniently, stepped out of her office by the time we'd arrived. I imagined her leaving a trail of nerves wherever she went; pacing the carpet to a dry thread in the head's office, maybe. It left us with too much time to be quiet – which came awkwardly, after the loud sobs and outbursts that had punctuated our journey. After her tears, Freya had turned back to rage – 'She'd better have some good fucking answers for us when we get there.' – and in a bid to keep my own tears bottled, I found I was running on the fumes of anger too. Though I tried to keep my face neutral, my quiet temper was simmering beneath the surface, which I hoped didn't show when I reached across to the chair where Freya sat next to me and grabbed her hand. She reciprocated and pressed her hot palm against my skin, but she didn't look at me. She was busy reading the certificates that were fixed to the left-hand wall; one photo frame after another that told visitors the qualifications of Mrs Day, listing her counselling expertise. I wondered who they were there for though. I couldn't see how any average teenager would care much, and it made me wonder how often Mrs Day – Deborah, according to the name plaque on the front of her desk – welcomed parents, or official bodies – *like police,* I auto-filled – into the office.

Freya and I were so deep in our own thoughts that we flinched in sync when the door opened. Freya didn't turn but I couldn't help myself. This was my first brush with the woman, and I hadn't yet created a photo-fit of what I was expecting her to look like. Curiosity got the better of me.

'Apologies for keeping you both waiting,' she said, when she saw me looking round, and I managed a smile. She wasn't at all what I had expected. From the certificates, I'd found myself waiting for an older woman with a curt face and a flat voice; one who would have already gone to the police, I decided, one who wouldn't have needed for us to arrive here and demand it. Instead, she was a young woman; no older than thirty-five, if I had to guess. Though she did creep around to her desk with her hands clasped and her face angled away from us, which made me think, *no, maybe you haven't been to the police at all.*

'With the head, were you?' Freya asked when the woman was seated, and Day managed a weak smile. 'I assume there's some official guidance on informing parents when their children are at risk from another student, Mrs Day–'

'Deborah, please,' the woman interrupted, and I saw Freya's expression turn to stone. 'I was with the head, yes, because he and I needed to discuss how to proceed with this matter. You'll know already that Connor's parents–'

'Oh,' Freya staged her own interruption, 'so you know exactly why we're here.'

Day looked at me as though she expected me to intervene. But instead I found my eyes drawn back to her many certificates. *Surely they gave you something on those many courses of yours...* I thought, and I couldn't find energy enough to correct the spite in my thinking. Freya needed a pound of flesh and in that moment, this woman's was as good as anyone else's. And it didn't matter how hard I tried to fight that thought away either.

'Connor's parents have been made aware of the matter, of course, which I can assume you already know.'

'Of course,' Freya parroted. 'And have the police been made aware?'

Again, Day looked at me, and I wondered what she thought my role was there, exactly. 'The head and I have discussed this matter extensively, and of course, we have a duty of care to the other students in the school.' Freya huffed then, but Day pressed on. 'We'll be notifying the police in the coming days, once we've had a follow-up meeting with Connor's parents. For now, he's suspended and the likelihood is that this will turn to an expulsion in the coming days too.'

There was a sadness in my belly then, chased down there by the thought that another young man might have lost his life now in an altogether different way.

'Why haven't you notified the police already, Deborah?' Freya leaned hard on the woman's name, as though to say, *if that* is *what the kids are calling you*. 'Given the situation, surely this is something they should have already been made aware of.' Freya's grief and sound logic were awkward bedfellows. I'd already proposed going to the police – and Kaleb had, too, Freya admitted earlier – but in that moment another possibility hit me: Freya hadn't wanted us to go to the police because she wanted someone else to. She wanted someone else to *care* enough to. She wanted to know after all this that now, at least, there was someone looking out for her boy.

Day shifted uncomfortably in her seat and the leather beneath her made a squeak-grinding noise. 'We were under the impression that Connor's parents would be going to the police themselves. That was the initial agreement, when we became aware of the situation at play here.'

I noted, then, how she avoided using their names. It struck me as strange and/or strategic, that she was putting Connor at the front of this conversation – without the veneer of his parents' names to hide behind. This was something happening *to him*; I thought she was reminding us. But of course, Freya was here because of something that had happened *to Ryan*, and there was no stopping her vengeance now.

'So I assume this is the first you've heard about a drug problem at your school?'

'Of course. If we'd known, we would have acted sooner.'

'If you'd acted sooner…' I started, then stopped when both women turned to me. They didn't need for me to complete the sentence; besides which, it likely wasn't my place to. But I couldn't help the beginnings of the accusation from spilling out.

Freya inched forward, then, so she could reach the desk. She tapped at it hard with her index finger as she spoke. 'I want to know whether Ryan ever came to you. He told me he did, once, when he was considering university choices. I want to know what was said; I want to know what you know.'

Day moved to reach into her trouser pocket, and then produced a small key. There was a mechanical click, somewhere out of sight, a slide and another click; what I assumed must be a drawer opening and closing. She dropped a slim file onto the desk and flashed a tight smile. 'I thought that might be the case, that it might be helpful to…' She petered out and looked between us both. 'There's nothing in here that pertains to what happened to Ryan, if I thought there was, please know that I would have shared this much sooner.'

'I'm not sure that's for you to judge, Mrs Day,' Freya answered. She leaned forward to snatch at the slim cardboard casing and then fell back into her seat with it. 'This is everything?' she asked, before it was even open.

'That's everything.' Day stole a glance at me then, a sly one that I might have missed, if I hadn't already been keeping an eye on her. And I thought I saw the beginnings of a frown. 'That's a copy, incidentally, and the police have their own, too, so if you want to take it home, perhaps, share it with your husband for…'

Freya's head snapped up. 'He isn't interested in this. I have Annie's support for it.' The comment landed like a hot rock in front of Day, something that might leave a mark on her palm if she were to reach out and touch it.

It felt as though she were trying to tell me something but I was clueless as to what. *Do you know, Freya? Has he told you after all?* The counsellor's office wasn't the place to press the issue, though, I knew that much. There was a dead-weight silence in the seconds that followed as Freya skimmed the file; loose papers collapsed into each other and I wondered how much of the contents she could even see. But then she paused and–

'He didn't want to go to university anymore?' She looked up at Day, who lowered her gaze. 'Is that what he said to you?' Her tone was louder that second time, and impossible for the counsellor to ignore.

She cleared her throat before answering. 'He told me that he had reservations about attending university, yes, and that his UCAS applications had been…' Again, she looked at me, and I wanted to remind her of whose side I was on. There shouldn't have been sides, of course. But there patently were. This woman held the key to unlocking part of Ryan that Freya hadn't been privy to; now, as his mother, she deserved it all. 'He told me they were a waste of his time, but that you and his father had insisted, and that you'd been happy to see him taking an interest in it all.'

'Which of course we had.' Freya sank in the chair then, her posture slinking down by a noticeable couple of inches. She ran a hand through her hair and then set her palm flat on her temple. 'Did he tell Jessica any of this?'

I shook my head. 'No, not that she's told me.' *And she would have done*, I wanted to add, but held back on it. Jess had been telling me more, but I knew, too, that she was still sad, still grieving – and most likely still protecting parts of Ryan. Besides which, she hadn't volunteered the information about drugs until she was pressed for it, I remembered then. 'We can ask her about it,' I reached across to grab her hand, the one still holding the folder, which meant I only managed an awkward grip, 'we can leave here and talk to her about it at home.'

An ill-timed interruption, there was the loud hum of a ringtone that cut through the office space, and I thought the suddenness of it had startled us all. Day breathed an audible sigh, of relief I assumed, and I pulled away from Freya to give her the space she needed to rifle through her handbag. She checked the screen for the ID of the caller and made a grunt-groan-grumble before depositing it back into her bag. The quiet among us all held until the caller had rung off.

'If there's anything else…' Day started, but she didn't complete the sentiment. We all knew how it ended; and I thought, too, we could likely take a guess at what Freya's response would have been. 'Of course, if there are any further developments with other students then we'll be letting you know as a matter of urgency.'

'After you've told their parents.' Freya made it sound like an unreasonable thing, but in context I couldn't decide whether it really was. 'Thanks for your time, Mrs Day.' She wedged the folder into her bag and stood. But I had my own question to poke with before I felt ready to leave.

'Bev Sykes,' I started and Day made a murmur of something, 'what type of relationship does she have with other students?'

'I couldn't possibly say.'

'Because you don't know?' I pushed.

'Because I'm not at liberty to.' She moved, as though to carry on speaking, but then stopped herself. Day leaned forward on the desk and took on an air of comfort; our imminent departure had clearly made it easier for her to play her role again. Still, she flashed a sympathetic expression and added, 'If this is about the incident the other day, with Jessica, I can tell you that the head has spoken with Beverley about it. Though of course, I can't add anything more.'

'Thank you.' I turned and set a hand on the bottom of Freya's back to guide her towards the door, as though helping an invalid. It was an automatic gesture. 'Come on, I'll take you home.'

We were hardly a handful of steps down the corridor when my own phone began to vibrate in the pocket of my jeans. I wrangled it free, all the while guiding Freya still, but when I checked the caller ID I could make an educated guess at who'd been calling her minutes earlier. I back-pocketed the handset, and decided it was best for me to ignore Kaleb too.

CHAPTER FIFTEEN

Freya invited me in but I politely declined. I didn't know what was waiting on the other side of that door. On the drive from the school I'd imagined a panicked Kaleb, wandering the halls, his hair sticking out at odd angles and his eyes shadowed with worry and lack of sleep. I didn't know whether that's how we would find him, and I was happy in my not knowing too. I only hoped that whatever his plan was, he would lower her down into it gently. The last thing Freya needed was another blow, I thought, even though I knew it was inevitable too. I kissed her cheek, hugged her too tight, and told her that I was going to walk home. When I arrived back, I was glad to see the darkness of the place. There was a low watt hum of light ebbing out from the edges of Jessica's curtains in her bedroom. Beyond that, I knew that I would at least get the quiet I so desperately needed after the day.

In the solace of the kitchen, with a heavy red wine in front of me, the rest of the weight landed brick by brick. The realisation that Ryan was doing drugs; that he was buying drugs from someone at school; that the university experience Freya had so keenly wanted for him had only been something he used to pacify her. One by one they all dropped on me a second time over like pennies landing in a fountain bowl. *Who were you, Ryan?* I wondered as I twirled the glass by its stem. I looked up to the ceiling then, and I thought that maybe Jessica wouldn't even know the right answer. Of course, no one knows who they are at seventeen; not really. We all might think we do but there were small plates and magnets, always shifting and dancing around each other, well into our twenties, if my own memories were anything to go by. And even then, nothing was set in stone.

'I wish you were here,' I said aloud but in a low voice. I had spent so much of the last few days wishing for Theo. It wouldn't lessen the grief, or the blows that each new piece of information brought with it, but it would have been a hand to hold in these dead hours; it would have been someone to turn to and ask, *Who even was this kid?* 'This kid, who we watched grow up.' I shook my head and took another sip.

The room was dimly lit by the small spotlights hidden beneath the high cupboards. There was a chill settling in, a draught that I couldn't place the source of, but every now and then something would nip at my ankles; a cold front sneaking into the room. I shifted to make sure the back door was shut; I unlocked it, even, with the express purpose of locking it again. And somehow, in the slight noise of that motion, I had missed Jessica coming downstairs. She was in the doorway when I turned and I felt my heart shudder-skip-settle. I lay a hand on my chest to feel its wing beat.

'It looks like an Edward Hopper painting in here,' she announced.

'That's quite the reference.'

She shrugged. 'We looked at him in literature, ekphrastic writing that was done from his paintings.' She trod into the room slowly as she spoke, as though laboured by the feelings I thought she must be carrying still. 'He has all of these paintings where women are alone, sad, thinking–'

'In that case, I'm offended.'

'But they're always beautiful, in their way.'

I smiled. 'Okay, you can take a seat at my sad table then.' And she did, but when I saw her staring into the bowl of my glass, I quickly added, 'But you're not having any of that.'

'That's fair.' There was no humour in her voice.

Somehow, since Ryan, my young girl had gained five to ten years; even her hair looked to have greyed. There were small shaded pillows under each eye where ill-feeling and lack of sleep were resting on her too.

'How's Freya?' she asked, now staring at the table.

It was a mighty fine question. I wondered again whether Kaleb had told her yet. *Had Ryan known about his father?* The idea ricocheted around inside me. It wasn't the first time I'd thought it. If Ryan was so adept at keeping secrets, had he been keeping Kaleb's? I wanted to ask Jessica if he'd ever said anything to her about that sort of thing – but there was *so* much I wanted to ask Jess about Ryan alongside that, and I couldn't decide where Kaleb's infidelity ranked around drug usage, university, truancy... I shook my head.

'I don't know, is the honest answer, sweetheart.'

'That's fair,' she repeated.

'We saw Connor today.'

Her head snapped up then. 'Did he tell you anything? Any news, I mean?'

'Ryan was doing drugs regularly, a lot of weed, by all accounts. We saw your counsellor at school too.'

'Deborah spoke to you about Ryan?'

I frowned. *Why are you on first-name terms with that woman?*

'She had a whole file on Ryan that she shared with Freya. She mentioned one or two things while we were there, too, about Ryan, and university...' I watched for her reaction. 'Had he told you he didn't want to go, sweetheart?' I leaned forward to reach for her hand but she dropped back in her chair to put a greater distance between us. 'There isn't a right or wrong answer, I only wondered... Well, I just wondered whether he'd been able to speak to you about it, that's all.'

She sniffed, nodded, stared at the table again. 'He told me he didn't want to go.' I left a quiet between us for a second or two in case there was more. Her mouth fidgeted then, her lips scrunched up to one side in a thoughtful expression. 'We argued about it, once or twice.'

I didn't like this steady drip-feed of information, and only when I asked the right question to elicit it. But in response I only said, 'I see,' for fear that anything more would make her clam up.

'I told him he was throwing his life away.' Despite the lack of humour earlier, she huffed a laugh now; a sad and defeated sound, though, maybe even a regretful one. 'It was always such a silly argument. Like, it never went anywhere, he never said he'd even think about it.'

'What did he say?'

'He said he'd get a job, stacking shelves, serving food, doing anything. He just wanted to earn some money while he worked things out. When he first said it, I went along with it. I always wanted to support him, you know? I always wanted him to have that from me.' She looked at me and behind the tired eyes and the wearied hair, I saw my young girl again. There were tears about ready to spill over in both of us. Still, I only murmured for her to carry on. 'I would have supported anything if he'd only spoken to me about it all more.'

'It sounds like you did the best you could, sweetheart.'

'It wasn't enough, though, was it? None of it was enough for him.'

I took a large mouthful of wine and thought, *Oh fuck it.* The bottle was still on the table. I trod across the room to fetch a second glass from the cupboard, set it down and poured a small splash of wine into it. Jessica watched me without saying anything. When I nudged the wine glass in front of her – only an inch, just a taste to ease the tension, or the sadness, or the feelings in between – she smiled, another sad expression on her, though, and took a small sip.

'I'm not encouraging drinking,' I said as I sat back in front of her, 'but Christ, if you don't deserve a little something to round the edge off all this.'

She took another sip without saying anything and then asked, 'Are you okay, Mum?'

I couldn't remember anyone asking in the days since Ryan. Someone must have, at some point, I told myself. But it wasn't a conversation that I could lay my hand to. *Had Kaleb asked?* I tried to remember but the whole meeting with him was blurred around the edges.

'It's very kind of you to ask, sweetheart.' I decided a non-answer was best. Because of course I wasn't okay. But I was okay enough. 'I'm more worried about you, and about Freya.'

'The police,' she started, but paused to take another sip of her drink, 'they aren't saying anything about who might have done it?'

'I don't think they know much at this stage still, sweetheart. But it is *very* early days for something like this too,' I parroted what the FLO had been telling Freya and Kaleb on repeat for days. She seemed to think it would comfort them but I could tell from their faces that it didn't have the desired effect; of course, how could it? It hadn't offered Jessica any comfort either, as I watched her shift uncomfortably in her seat, her eyes still hooded, hidden from my own. She hadn't been able to look Freya in the eye since it had happened, and I'd noticed in passing days that she was starting to struggle with me too. *Is that grief?* I wondered, *Is that shame, that she's here and Ryan isn't?* The thought gripped me like a vice around the throat and I felt the need to clear it; I half-coughed to shift the feeling but it was still there, bearing down, tightening.

'Do you think they'll find the person who did it?'

I sighed. 'I bloody hope so.'

There was a long and heavy silence, then, as though a weighted blanket were draped across the room – though it did nothing to ease the anxious buzz of the space. Jessica took measured sips of her wine, though I noticed those sips were getting closer together. Meanwhile, I emptied my glass in a swift improper glug. She said nothing, but I noticed her looking at me while I poured another inch or two. I wasn't setting a good example, I knew that. But I was also exhausted and worried and– One hundred other adjectives that in no way did justice to the mess of our lives now. Freya's child had been murdered, I thought it on a loop like a broken disc player wedged on the same track. The reality of it all quilted around me, and I felt my shoulders shudder as the sob arrived there first. Before I could swallow it back, a moan fell out of me and a tear escaped each eye and my elbows were on the table cradling my head and–

'I'm so sorry, Mum.'

'Sweetheart,' I looked up at her and hoped the tears would ebb for long enough, 'this isn't your fault, at all.' I reached across for her hand and that time she didn't pull away; she looked at me, too, straight in eye, and I said again, 'It isn't your fault.' Stress fell on every word and as though exhausted by the energy of it, my chest juddered out the breath that followed. I wondered how much feeling must be lodged in there.

'It is my fault, though, Mum. I'm the reason–'

I squeezed her hand tight to stop her. 'You're not the reason for anything.'

'You don't understand.' She shook her head.

'Help me to understand then. Why do you think this is your fault?'

Her eyes were heavy with tears that looked fixed in place. I was desperate for her to blink, to release it all. But she was staring at me with a fixed expression that I recognised from somewhere else too: stolen biscuits; misspent pocket money; a broken curfew.

'Because I did it, Mum.' She blinked and my stomach fell through me. 'That's why it's my fault. That's why I'm the reason.'

PART 2

JESSICA

CHAPTER SIXTEEN

I didn't want to be *that* girl: the one who texts and checks the WhatsApp ticks and checks the 'message read at' whatever time. But Christ, how long does it take to reply to a message? Ryan should have been in his Business Studies class but there was no way of knowing whether he actually was; not until the next lesson kicked in anyway, when he would be in a free period. Well, if he were in school that is, it would be a free period. Around me, the girls were all checking their own phones, swapping their stories, moaning about their love interests: Becky and Heather had had their first argument as a couple and they were letting us know, by sitting on opposite sides of their usual sofa; Sally was about ready to kick Myles to the kerb (though she didn't know why, exactly, more than having a feeling it was the right time); meanwhile, Lynda and Louise were both resorting to dating apps, having decided the boys at school were too close to 'shitting where you eat'.

'What does that even mean?' Sally asked. 'Why are you shitting on them?'

'Not literally,' Lynda answered.

'Pervert,' Louise added, without looking up. 'This one looks cute enough. What do you think?' She held her screen up for the rest of us to see and I tried to engage, tried to care. But Ryan still hadn't read my message.

'Still nothing?' Heather asked me in a low voice and I shook my head.

'Kick him to the kerb!' Sally added.

My stomach dipped. 'That's your answer to everything.'

'Not everything. Just men.'

'Seconded,' Becky chimed in and there was a low snigger from around the group. She had come out as a lesbian when she was twelve and, despite what her parents had thought, she'd since then gone very far out of her way to prove that it in fact wasn't a phase. 'On a serious note, ladies,' she said, changing her tone, 'Jess loves Ryan and we all know Ryan loves Jess. If they want to work at it, they should. That's how it works when you love someone, isn't it?' She cocked an eyebrow in Heather's direction and I felt her physically relax next to me. There's nothing like a public olive branch to melt a young girl's heart; *so I hear at least,* I thought as I sighed and checked my phone, again.

'Give me that thing.' Louise clicked her fingers in my direction. 'I'm cutting you off.' I handed over the handset. 'You can have it back at lunchtime as long as you're not mental between now and then.'

I laughed. 'I can't be mental. I don't have a phone to keep checking.'

'Well then, I guess you'll get it back,' Lynda answered as she swiped right, left, left, left– 'Fuck me, this is dire.'

'Can someone cut you two off?' I already felt more relaxed. It was Schrödinger's text now; the lesser known version. 'Wouldn't it be nice if we *all* had a break from our phones?'

'Listen to this one,' Sally nodded at me, 'three seconds without her phone and she's on a technology cleanse.'

'Speaking of cleansing, anyone noticed how freakin' good my

skin looks?' Becky leaned in to show the group her face, that we'd been staring at intermittently throughout the entire conversation without commenting on it. But once it had been highlighted to us, we fell over ourselves to see who could compliment her first, and from there spilled a round table discussion of the products we were all using; the ones that helped a hormone breakout and the ones that made them worse. And I tried to look unfazed whenever one of the girls replied to a text or checked Instagram or–

'Christ, I can't stand her, you know?'

My head shot up to see who Heather was referring to. There weren't many people in the school – in the world even – who Heather passionately hated. But her and Bev Sykes had a long-standing rivalry that dated back to Bev outing Heather to the entire sixth-form common room last year. Heather hadn't let it go – so neither had any of us.

'H, don't even look at her,' Becky said, suddenly closing the distance along the sofa. *If only all wars were so easily won*, I thought as I watched the two huddle together. It took me a beat longer to realise that if Bev were here that must mean the period had ended though – somewhere in the middle of our break-up and make-up tip talk.

I craned round to the door of the common room just in time for–

'Babe!'

Ryan rushed to me like he hadn't seen me for days. He stood behind me and threw his arms around my shoulders and I pulled in a greedy inhale of the feelings – and the smell of pot.

'Ladies,' he greeted the girls as he straightened up, 'how are we all? Still chewing boys up and spitting them out on the pavement?'

'Not all of us,' Becky answered, which prompted further sniggering.

I tipped my head back to talk to Ryan. 'I didn't know whether you were in today.' Even from the awkward angle, he was the most beautiful boy I'd seen in my fucking life.

He kissed my forehead. 'I missed Critical Thinking but made it for Business.'

'Don't those two kind of go together?' Sally answered.

'I wouldn't be so sure if you look at the state of the economy right now, Sally,' he answered, and we all laughed. For as long as I could remember, Ryan had been the funniest boy in any room. Things had shifted recently – since he'd started smoking more – and there were times when instead of the funniest, he was the most lucid, or the least interested. So I tried to bask in the glow of him then, and enjoy the moment as he landed in the sofa space next to me and wrapped an arm around my shoulders. He pulled me to him and fixed me there.

'Mum and Dad are out tonight. Coming over?' he asked, and kissed my head a second time. I nodded and tucked myself in further against him. We'll have time together, I thought, we'll have time together, and we'll have sex, and he won't smoke. And it'll set everything just right.

CHAPTER SEVENTEEN

It had started to hurt after we'd had sex, and I couldn't work out whether it was me – there was something wrong, down there – or with us – Ryan was doing something differently too. He'd mentioned porn once or twice already; not as something we could watch together, but he made it all too clear that he was watching it alone, and I didn't really know what I was meant to do with the info-dump of that. I didn't know what to do with the discomfort either. So instead I lay there with my head against his chest and I let a happy sigh slip out while he ran his fingertips over the spot between my shoulder blades, and I resolved to deal with any discomfort by having a long bath when I got home. There was music humming in the background but it was too quiet for me to know exactly what it was. Apart from that, the house was in complete silence – and it was lovely. I couldn't remember the last time my own home had felt like it. For a one-woman band Mum could make a shitload of noise, and the hush of being with Ryan – being *anywhere* with Ryan, but being in bed with him was a bonus – felt like an energy shot. I didn't tell him that though; I didn't want to tell him anything that would make me sound… Well, like I loved him as much as I did. He didn't need to know that.

'Hey,' he hugged me closer to him, 'where's your head at?'

I huffed a laugh. 'I'm here. What do you mean?'

'I don't know, you seemed miles away.' He shifted then, to get a proper look at my face. I stared up at him, unwilling to move from my warm spot on his right pec. 'Was it okay, the… Was it okay?'

He looked desperately worried and even though I felt horrible for it, I couldn't help but think, *Good, because a little self-doubt wouldn't be so bad on you right now*. I didn't even know where the thought came from. True, Ryan had been a touch different lately, but I would never have wished insecurities on him. If anything, it was my job to take those away. I shook the snide thought out of my head and smiled up at him.

'Babe, it was perfect.' He seemed to settle then, but still I added, 'It always is with you.'

'Good. I want it to be good.'

Ryan and I had been each other's firsts; we'd been fifteen and it was awful. So awful, in fact, that in the minutes afterwards we both sat on separate sides of the bed, our feet hanging over our respective edges, our backs to each other and our heads hung low. There was too much blood and not enough time, and nothing that either of us had read had prepared us for those things. Ryan's friends had told him he wouldn't last long, meanwhile, my friends had told me that I might not bleed – but the knock-on effect of those two elements clanging together left us both worried and sad and, I think, a bit ashamed. In the end, so much silence had passed between us that I quietly took myself for a shower to wash everything away. When I'd got back to Ryan's room he wasn't there, and I eventually found him downstairs making pancakes and singing along to whatever happened to be on the radio at the time. We didn't talk about that first time, not then or since, but it felt like we'd spent the last two years making up for it with what felt, to me, like bloody fantastic sex. Until about two months ago…

'Are you hungry?' he asked eventually. 'I'm starving.'

'You always are after!' I poked him in the tummy. 'What do you fancy?'

'Now there's an offer.' He moved so fast that I didn't register what was happening until he was on top of me, his fingers wiggling against my ribs, then my tummy, then back to my ribs, and I squirmed and laughed and squirmed some more. I was deadly ticklish, everywhere; it had always been one of his favourite things.

Soon, though, the tickling ceased, and Ryan rested with his head against my stomach. He kissed from belly button down to thighs and I swallowed all the soft noises that were trying to burst out of me. But then the kisses stopped.

'Fucking hell.' He was kneading at my thigh muscle. 'Jesus, Jess, did *I* do that?'

I shot up to inspect my leg then, and found Ryan staring hard at the beginnings of a bruise; black and purple bubbles under the skin that looked like they might form the shape of an apple once the colours came to the surface. I put my hand over it.

'It doesn't matter.' I smiled. Because it really didn't matter. 'These things happen, babe.' *Especially lately…* I guided his head up towards mine and kissed one cheek, then the other, then his forehead. 'Come on, are you going to feed me or what?'

'What are we in the mood for?' He moved off the bed and grabbed his T-shirt from the floor.

'Hm, Chinese? We could order it in, or walk round and get it.' I started to ferret for my own clothes then. 'How long will your parents be out, do you think?' You never quite knew with Freya and Kaleb. If they were getting along, they could be out all night; if they weren't, then the front door was likely to slam back on its hinges any minute. Mum always talked about them like they were so happy and I never had the heart to correct her but Christ, this house could tell some stories.

'I think it's a late one. Mum has dragged him to that art gallery thing in town. Lots of potential clients there, she thinks. You know what she's like.' He rolled his eyes and then checked his phone, for the time I guessed. 'Hey, I've got a cracker of an idea.' Ryan leaned forward and kissed my bare knees before I had the chance to pull my jeans back on. 'How about we order in, then in the time it'll take for food to get here, we can have a little treat…'

He pulled open the top drawer of his bedside table and reached to the back of the space. I knew what was coming, but I still felt my tummy drop when he turned round: joint and lighter in hand.

'Babe…' he said, and I wondered what face I must have made. 'Come on, it's just a little pick-me-up. You haven't even tried it.'

'Because I don't want to try it,' I snapped. 'If you want to pump your body full of that, that's on you, but I'm not, I'm just not–'

'All right, I get it,' he cut me off. 'Do you want to order food?' He crossed the room to open the window and perched on the ledge, then sparked up like nothing had passed between us. 'Just get a double portion of whatever you want. I'll eat anything in about thirty minutes.'

And he laughed. He actually fucking laughed!

Something in me snapped then, like a thread had been pulled too tight. I stood up from the bed and pulled my clothes straight. 'I'm going to eat at home.'

He looked at me, narrowed his eyes, and shrugged. I don't know what I'd been expecting, but when he said, 'Okay,' I felt as though I could double over with bad feeling. But my mother had raised me better than that. So I slipped out of the room, rushed downstairs, and made a point of *not* slamming the front door behind me.

CHAPTER EIGHTEEN

Sally was lying on my bed with her head dangling over one edge, giving me an upside-down view of her face. In the two minutes where I hadn't been looking at the group chat, she'd sent around an announcement to let us all know she'd gone ahead and chucked Myles. 'He cried, can you believe that?' she asked me then, and I cocked an eyebrow at her. 'Don't look at me in that tone of voice, woman, we'd been together for five minutes. Who cries after five minutes?'

'You were together for three months.'

'That's what I said.'

I laughed. 'Did you leave things on good terms, after the crying?'

'We'll stay friends, yada yada, just isn't the right time for a relationship, yada yada, it's not him, it's– Are you listening?'

'To your break-up script?'

'It isn't a script!'

'Really? Because it sounds remarkably similar to everything you said to Mark when–'

'Mark was cheating on me, in case you've forgotten. Which reminds me,' she threw herself upright and reached to the floor for her bag. In the pause, I felt something angry grip my stomach; an untrained puppy with a new chew toy. 'I brought you a lifeline. You don't have to use it.' She launched something in my direction and instinctively I put my hands out to catch it.

'You brought me a phone?'

'I brought you *the* phone.'

'Oh, Sally...'

'Don't *oh, Sally*, me. Do you want to know what he's doing or not?'

The phone was a handset that Louise introduced to the group as many as five years ago, when boyfriends became a much more serious matter. Louise was convinced that her boyfriend – the boy's name wasn't even logged in my memory, that's how many there'd been since – was seeing other girls. At the time, she'd brought a cheap throwaway phone complete with a new SIM card so she could start texting him as someone else. Like a Greek chorus, we all predicted tragedy and told her that nothing good would come from it – which was true, given that it turned out he actually was cheating on her, or at least, he was willing to cheat with whoever it was he thought he was texting. And of course, that did nothing to dissuade Louise from back-pocketing her masterplan – and the handset – and reserving it for future use, which she saw as inevitable. Since then all the girls had used it at one time or another – apart from me.

'Do you think he's cheating?'

'Honestly?' she said, screwing her mouth to one side, and I felt the angry puppy tug on me again. 'I don't see Ryan as the type. But even if he isn't cheating, texting someone he doesn't really know that well might loosen that tongue of his, so at least you'll get *some* idea of what's happening when you're not there.'

I sighed. 'I really don't like this plan.'

'Baby doll, *none* of us have ever *liked* this plan. But sometimes...' She shrugged. 'I don't know, sometimes there aren't other options, are there?'

I juggled the phone between my hands for a second and then dropped it on the desk. 'He's smoking weed still.'

'I know.' When I shot her a look she added, 'He stinks of it.'

'How his parents haven't noticed...'

'Have you thought of telling them?'

'Are you mad?' It was my knee-jerk response. But the truth was, I had thought of telling them. More than once when Freya had been here chattering away with Mum, I'd thought of it. It wasn't the easiest of things to drop into conversation, though, and while I loved Freya, I also wasn't sure I knew her well enough to know what her reaction to something like that would be. Would she tell Ryan that *I* was the one who'd told her? Would he guess? It all felt too much of a risk, especially when I wanted Ryan closer, not pulling away. Betraying his trust didn't feel like the right step. I looked at the phone again then, and replayed the thought: *Betraying his trust is a terrible idea*.

The front door slammed downstairs and seconds later Mum shouted up. 'Jess?'

'Up here, Mum.'

'Hi, Annie!' Sally added to the percussion of Mum's footsteps climbing the stairs. 'We're up here moaning our way through the best years of our lives,' she said as Mum rounded my door and stepped into the room.

Mum laughed then. 'Well I'm glad you're using your time wisely. Sweetheart, are you in or out tonight?'

'In,' I answered, too quickly. I couldn't see Ryan, that much I knew; not with that phone weighing on my young heart. 'Sally is staying for dinner.'

'I am?' She looked at me, and nodded. 'I am.'

'Beautiful. What do you girls fancy?'

'Oh, Annie, now there's a question.'

She laughed again. 'Sall, remember that I know your mother.'

'In that case, I'm easy.'

'Again, Sally, remember that I know your mother.' The joke

caught us both off-guard and Sally and I erupted with a howl. 'I know, I know, I'm embarrassing.' Mum flapped a hand in my direction.

'Not even, Annie, you're hilarious.'

'I try.' Mum curtsied. 'Spag bol?'

'Perfect,' Sall and I said in unison. 'Do you want some help, Mum?'

'Not at all, sweetheart,' she was already halfway out the room, 'keep on bemoaning whatever it was. I'll give you a shout when it's done.'

'Your mum is so cool, you know?'

I nodded. 'Yeah, she's kind of the best.'

CHAPTER NINETEEN

Ryan had skipped school again. I didn't know where he was or what he was doing – or who he was doing it with. And I'd poured an immeasurable amount of my shitty feelings from that into a sports training session that had left me with a bloodied knee and a bite mark on the inside of my cheek from having made hard contact with another player on the field. I was so fucking done with everything about the day. I slammed cupboard after cupboard to find something to eat but, despite my hunger, every space looked like an abyss, and I hated myself the tiniest bit for being *that* girl again: the one that stares into the distance waiting for a text tone. I'd even left my phone on silent since school specifically so I could justify checking it again: *Maybe he* has *texted me but I've missed it because my phone isn't on vibrate.* I checked again and then threw the handset across the kitchen work surface when I saw the blank screen. Mum tutted from somewhere behind me.

'What's going on with you?' she asked, while I was facing off against another cupboard of uncooked pasta and bottled sauces.

'Fucking sports practice,' I lied, 'it's just a waste of fucking time, isn't it?' It was an easy get-out; I'd never been a sports person, and the fact that I was losing an hour of revision every week so I could practice a string of sports I had no interest or talent for just made it all the more frustrating. *Nothing to do with your boyfriend being a shit.* I shook the thought away but not before I'd had the chance to berate myself for it. He wasn't a shit, but I was pretty convinced he wasn't behaving like a prince either.

That's why earlier in the day I'd cracked and texted him from the phone Sally had given me; she was the only friend who knew I was using it. The text only said, *What's your plan for tonight?* I'd heard other girls in the common room talking about a bonfire party – *more like bin-fire party,* I'd thought at the time – and I wondered whether it would be the type of thing to lure Ryan back on school grounds for the evening. Behind the football field there was a patch of land that the school owned. It had been bought with the intention of breaking in a new building but rumour was they hadn't raised the money for it. It was secluded, though, well enough for a huddle of teenagers to hug themselves warm and drink spirits from a bottle, if that was your thing; though it had never been mine.

Whatever the plan for the party, Ryan still hadn't replied to the text.

'That's a tongue you've on you there, missus.'

'I'm sorry, Mum. It just turned into a really long... Well, just a pig of a day, that's all.' I grabbed an open bag of jelly babies that was lying on the side from Sally's visit in the days before. When there were three green ones wedged uncomfortably close together, I started to chew – and I started to wonder, too, when I'd last checked the dummy phone for a reply...

'Why don't I fix you actual dinner, rather than whatever crap you're going to pull out of that sweet box?'

I turned around and smiled a jelly grin.

'What are we having?'

'Well, I'm having pizza with Freya. You can have...'

'Pizza on my own?'

'Order in, charge my Uber Eats.'

I showered her with compliments, swallowed another three sweets and turned my attention to the fridge. There was a chocolate milkshake in there that I'd been saving for a shitty occasion.

'How was Ryan today?'

Milkshake ran down my nose as I spluttered into the drink and I had to cough hard to clear my throat. It might have been an innocent question. Mum was a fan of small talk, and she might, logically, have been trying to shift the conversation onto something she thought was safer than sports practice. But something in her tone told me it was more likely that–

'You already know he wasn't in school today, Mum.'

I heard her sigh. 'You're a good kid, Jess.'

'So is he.' I turned to face her, then, and she kicked out the chair that was opposite her at the table. I took the cue, but not before putting my bad-day milkshake back into the fridge and pouring a second drink to take over with me. I didn't know whether it was the thought of maybe lying to Mum, or being grilled by her, but suddenly my tongue was dry paper.

She waited until I was sitting before she asked, 'Is he doing this a lot?'

'I don't know whether I'd say *a lot*.'

She made a noise like she was trying to laugh but it didn't carry right. 'More than once?'

'Yes, more than once.'

'Weekly?'

'Mum, isn't this a conversation to have… Wait, no. This *isn't* a conversation to have. It's between him and *his* mum.' She narrowed her eyes at me. 'And you know I'm right.'

'Nice try, but his mum happens to be my best friend. Do I need to be talking to Freya about this?'

I downed what was left of my drink. 'Honestly? I don't know.

Ryan... he's going through something, I think. Well, I know. I just don't know what it is.'

'Then how do you know he's going through something at all?'

Because he's screening my texts for days? Because he's constantly high? Because sex with him hurts?

'I just know.'

'Okay, well is *that* something I should be talking to Freya about?'

I leaned back in my chair. I wanted to be as far away from this conversation as I could be, but I knew it wouldn't help anything. 'To say what? My worry-wart daughter thinks there's something wrong with your son because he isn't as keen he used to be?'

She made a face that said, *Ah.* 'Is that what this is actually about?'

'Mum...'

'I'm not pushing,' she held her hands up in a defensive gesture, 'but we're already talking about it, so we may as well get everything out at once rather than stop-start-stop over the next... I don't know, however many weeks or months or... You think Ryan has lost interest?'

Once uncorked, it all came spilling out across the table. I told Mum that I was worried, that Ryan was more distant than he used to be, that I didn't think he'd *lost*-lost interest, but that something had certainly changed. I left some blank spaces, too, most importantly the fact that he was only talking about universities to keep everyone around him happy, me included, sometimes, I thought – and his main concern these days looked to be how often he could get baked under his parents' roof without anyone noticing it. 'He just has life worries, I guess,' I said in the end, not knowing how else to wrap a bow on the information dump.

There was a long pause before she answered, 'I won't tell Freya anything.'

Relief rushed out of me. 'Thank you, Mum.'

'But I do think that you should talk to Ryan about all of this, Jess. You're a kind and mature young woman for being astute to your partner's needs. He'll appreciate that, if not now, then certainly a few years down the line when he wishes for someone to magically know what he's thinking.'

'None of that,' I waved a hand at her reassurances, 'sounds sexy to me.'

And that, thankfully, looked to be the conversation-stopper I'd been searching for. We changed the subject then, and she walked me through her latest work project until it was time for her to disappear upstairs and get ready to leave for Freya's. It wasn't until she was leaving, though – 'Waiting on Ryan?' – that gears started to shift again, but in an ill-fitting way; an awkward understanding fell together when she reminded me to take my keys because, *She thinks I'm going somewhere...*

When she slammed the door behind her I finally thought to check the dummy phone; my own had remained blank all afternoon. But when I keyed in the passcode to the other handset there it was, hovering, offensively bright and too familiar in tone: *Soz whos this? Party. School. You in?*

CHAPTER TWENTY

I didn't reply to his message. Instead, I did the only logical thing I could think to do, which was to angry-eat my way through an entire pizza. I glanced at my own phone periodically, between slices, like it was some kind of palate cleanser. By the time I'd finished eating he still hadn't texted me. And then whatever 'logic' there was it dissipated quickly, because I was putting on my black jogging bottoms and then pulling on a black hoodie, grabbing gloves even, as though the pizza had turned me into an expert in espionage. Though the gloves were more practical than strategic; it was going to be bloody freezing when I stepped out the front door. I eyed myself in Mum's mirror. My hair was pulled back into a tight bun and hidden beneath the hood of my jumper and I thought, *I could be anyone.* Which I suppose had been the point. I had every intention of going to the party but no intention of being seen, and I reasoned that black was the best colour blend for the mission I was on. That's exactly how I moved, too, like I was on a mission. I slammed the front door behind me with a brute force, double-locked it like Mum had always told me to do, and then I marched in the direction of the school.

On the fifteen minute walk there I called Sally – who didn't answer – and Louise – who only answered to hurriedly explain she was on a date, but was I okay?

No, I wanted to double over in the middle of the street and scream it, no, I wasn't okay, and I needed a friend in my not okay-ness. But instead I said, 'Oh my God, of course. I'm so sorry. Let me know when you're home safe.' Then I disconnected the call before she had the chance to ask any questions – or sense the tension in my voice that seemed glaring even to me.

The school itself was in darkness. There was a small scrap of light from the dull lamps over the football field, though, which was enough for me to cross the space and get to the party on the other side. People must have been feeling risky, too, or drunk enough already, because I could hear their music humming across the airwaves between me and the space. I pushed through the hedgerows – a deliberate gap already carved out by partygoers – and stepped into the busy landscape. There was a small fire in the centre of it where some people were huddled. But there were factions, too, made up of people I recognised and some who I didn't. *Are you* all *from our school?* I wondered then. *Or are these parties that bit bigger than I realised?* It made it easy to stay anonymous, though, as I skirted around the groups and said nothing to anyone along my way. En route, I checked both my phone and the fake phone again: Ryan hadn't contacted either. And even though I was relieved to see he wasn't texting this unknown person, there was a horrid and uncomfortable wave of fury that started to ebb and flow in my tummy that he hadn't taken the time to text me either, even though I'd texted him three times by then.

I couldn't decide whether my actions and reactions were in proportion anymore. *Should I be here?* I skirted further, past another group. Though if it were Mum who I was talking to, I knew already she'd say if I was asking the question then I probably sensed the answer. But I shook that logic anyway. I tried for some kind of middle ground, some sort of reasoning with myself, and I made a promise that if I hadn't spotted him within five minutes, then I would leave. If I didn't see–

But of course, I saw. Or rather, I heard.

'Fuck off! Give it back.'

Ryan was wrestling with another boy, but in a playful way. And when a plume of smoke loomed over his head, I realised what he'd been wrestling for was a cigarette. *But it's probably not just a cigarette, is it?* Ryan took two thirsty drags, smoke bellowing out of him each time, before passing the joint across to Beverley fucking Sykes. *Of course, she's here.* Bev took her own measure and then passed it along, and this continued like a teenage re-imagining of pass the parcel. I tried to place the faces of the group while lingering far enough away. And it was easy enough to linger, with how many people were there, but that meant it was harder to listen in, too, harder to guess at what Ryan was saying while he staggered and smiled and– *Continued not replying to my fucking messages.* There came the same wave as before, this time accompanied by nausea.

I put my hand over my mouth and paused for a second. A second was all it took for everything to shift, though, when a new member of the group bounded up to my boyfriend...

She was taller – taller than me, and fractionally taller than Ryan – and even though I couldn't get an altogether clear look at her face, I could tell that she was pretty. It might have been her demeanour that gave it away: the hot-girl strut.

Ryan gave her a hug that lasted for too long, and when she pulled away from him she lingered. Something passed between them, words rushed from mouths to ears and then a belch of laughter erupted out of him. They touched hands in an overfamiliar way, too, not quite a handshake but more like a caress. She leaned in to kiss his cheek, and he laughed again, then she bounded away. It could have stopped there, too; everything could have settled down easily enough if–

'Ryan, where are you going?' someone shouted.

'For a walk,' he hollered back, and then he abandoned the group and headed for the same direction as the woman with the hot-girl strut.

I gave him a minute head-start before I followed. I hoped that I wouldn't catch him up – or rather, I hoped that he'd turn around and go back to the group of stoners he'd left behind. But he didn't. He paused for high fives and hugs along his way out of the field, but there was no stopping him on the journey to wherever he was heading; he walked with a hearty amount of determination for someone who was so clearly baked out of their mind. And I followed at a safe distance; I kept a clear ten metres between us while I stalked him back through the same hedgerows I'd used minutes before. But when I spotted him halfway across the field, pulling what looked like a phone out of his pocket, something just –'Ryan, what the absolute fuck!' – snapped.

He turned, staggered, squinted. 'Jessie?'

'Don't, just fucking don't.'

'What are you even…' He gestured to the space around us. 'You're here?'

'I am. Surprised much? On account of you not having invited me.' I was close enough to shove him then, a light push, but he was off-balance enough to stagger backwards with it. I'd never done anything like it before but nothing in me felt bad about doing it now – and I thought, from the look on Ryan's face, we were both just as surprised by the gesture. 'Who's the girl?'

'Who's the– What? What girl?'

'The girl I *literally* just saw you with.' I pointed back to where we'd come from. 'The girl with the pretty-girl walk?' He looked confused, and all I could think then was, *The girls would know* exactly *what I meant*. 'You two were…' I waved a hand around in search for the right word but I couldn't find one that would hold their intimacy. 'The girl!'

'Jesus, Jess, were you *spying*?'

'Don't do that. Don't make this a me problem, Ryan.'

'But you were? You fucking were. You crazy–'

'Don't do that!' And I shoved him again, harder that time.

He staggered and huffed something that nearly sounded like a laugh. 'I'm not doing this with you, Jess, not while you're like this.'

'Not while *I'm* like this? When you're the one goggle-eyed on pot?'

'Okay then, not while *I'm* like this. Whatever.' Then a real laugh escaped, a full and curt, HA, and I was desperate for him to feel ashamed by it, to retract it even. I wanted him to clasp his hands to his mouth and be wide-eyed with embarrassment and to fall to his fucking knees and– 'Jess, I'm going home and we're going to talk this shit out tomorrow.'

'No, we aren't.'

'Okay then, you're right, let's not talk it out at all, let's just–'

'Tell me who the girl is, Ryan.'

'Jess.' He took a step backwards as though trying to create a safe distance. But in this wide open space there wasn't one. I stepped forwards. 'She's just a girl. She's a girl who I… She's just a girl, okay?'

But it had slipped out; there was a half-formed sentence strung between us, and I needed for him to fill in the blank. 'She's a girl who you what?'

He ferreted around in the pocket of his jeans and found something slim, which he held up for me to see. 'She's a girl who I buy from, okay?' It was weed; he was showing me a small bag of weed. 'Every now and then I splash out on some good stuff and she's a girl from out of town who sells. Okay?'

No, I thought, *nothing about this is okay*. 'Why did you look so friendly with her? Why did you look like…' I didn't know what they'd looked like. All I knew in those brittle moments was that I didn't believe him – and I was right not to.

'Jess, look,' he came closer then, which felt like a bold act after his previous distancing, 'I'm going to tell you this, and then I'm going to go home and sleep this shit off, and we're going to finish this tomorrow. Is that a deal?'

No. 'Okay.' My fists tightened inside the pockets of my jumper and I felt my jaw release a low crack; I hadn't even realised I was clenching my teeth. 'Okay,' I repeated, though I was bouncing on my heels by then, as though readying to enter the ring – even though it felt a little like I'd already stepped into it.

'We hooked up, once. She and I, we...' He waved a hand around. 'You know.'

'No, Ryan, I don't.' I wanted to hear him say; I *needed* to hear–

'Fucked. We fucked, like, one time, Jess, and it was good and great and...'

He kept talking. He told me too much. And after that, everything got too loud.

PART 3

ANNIE

CHAPTER TWENTY-ONE

The ground was winter wet, but I'd brought a blanket with me. It was fleeced, with a waterproof underlining; the kind that crinkled uncomfortably if you shifted about on it too much. I'd forgotten I had it in the car, but when I drove, as though on automatic, to the crematorium I was relieved to have it with me. I laid it out in front of Theo's headstone and tried to remain mindful of the neighbouring ones, and then I sat cross-legged in front of him. My mobile phone lay between us and within seconds it hummed another missed call from Jessica, but I just–

'Theo, I can't,' I whispered. Then I leaned forward and set my palm flat on the cold of him, and imagined instead that it was his chest. I imagined I could feel the angry thrum of his heartbeat beneath the warmth of his skin, and the smell of him as he pulled me into an enveloping hug. He always wore Calvin Klein Defy and for years I'd kept a bottle on my dressing table.

'It's probably gone off by now,' I said, still in a whisper.

I imagined his quiet laugh then, and how he might lower his head to kiss the crown of mine, and how he might tell me a kind lie – 'It'll work out, Annie, we're going to work all this out.' –

even though, of course, there was no way of knowing when or how or if anything about this might work out.

I kept my hand pressed against the cool stone, leaning harder into it, and tried to paint this as though Theo was alive still. He might make tea – 'It's never made anything worse.' – or maybe I would. And we would sit at the kitchen table, each of us cradling a mug that we couldn't stand to drink from. But we'd need the warmth after the shock of it, and that might be when one of us would stand and say something like, 'Scotch, that's warm, and it's better for shock.' We'd replace our mugs with squat tumblers, and we would hold hands across the table, and we might remember back to a time when the worst thing our daughter had done was to take money from my purse without asking. 'Even though she admitted to it before you even noticed,' Theo might remind me, and I would nod in a sad agreement.

'What are we going to do, Annie?'

I might huff and answer to that. 'Why do you think I have any bright ideas?'

He would say nothing about the snap in my voice, or the sharp teeth of me. Theo would only clasp my hand and then we'd resume the discomfort of quiet. Though of course, we'd both be listening for the sounds of life overhead where our daughter was skulking; perhaps trying to listen to anything we might have to say for her. But there was nothing; there would have been nothing either of us could say.

Crematoriums and gravesides, I had learned, were notoriously quiet places; you could guarantee a secret would stay there. After a few moments of contact, I brought both hands to a rest in my lap and I sat there with my husband, much how we might have sat across from each other while we tried to swallow the bitter pills our daughter had just spat across the floor like a child rejecting their vegetables from dinner. Once she'd started, everything had come tumbling out.

A chill moved through me at the memory, and the incomplete details. I hadn't stayed for her entire explanation, because what parent could have?

'You probably could have.' I sighed and stared at the gold writing of the grave. *That really needs redoing*, I thought, then, *Is that a normal thought to have in this moment?* 'Is there a normal thought at all to have in this moment?'

That, at least, was an authentic question; that was the type of question my husband or I might have asked across the kitchen table. Along with questions like, 'How could she...' and 'Do you think that's why...'

'Along with questions like, who do I tell?' I asked Theo and I hoped, by the power of whoever it was that snatched my husband from me in the first place, that an answer might come. I thought that if any allowances could be made for a dead loved one returning to you, this may tick some if not all of the requirement boxes. Though of course, if that were the case, I dreaded to think what Ryan might tell his mother if he were allowed to step back into his body for the briefest of moments: 'Jessica, Jessica did it,' he might say. And for the first and last time ever, I was grateful Theo wasn't there – and wasn't able to be.

Jessica had sobbed her small wild heart out and explained everything as it had happened, or as she could remember it happening. And when we reached the point of blunt force trauma I had shouted, 'Just stop!' across the kitchen, and she had stared back at me like I'd slapped her – which, admittedly, was something else I'd considered doing, for the first time in my parenthood. I hadn't been able to stay any longer but even now, even with Theo, I knew I would have to run home; I would have to decide what to do with our child. After nearly eighteen years of protecting her, it had never occurred to me that she might become the thing others needed to be protected from. The very thought of it sent a shudder through my chest wall; multiple muscles contracting at once and juddering out in an angry animal cry.

'Fucking hell, Theo, what do I do? Who do I tell?'

Of course, there came no answer. But seconds later there was a small and tentative, 'Annie?' and my head shot up as though someone had stunned me with a sharp jab to the back of the neck.

'I'm sorry, I… It's Josie, Josie Leach.'

I half-recognised the name but I mostly recognised the face. Or rather, I recognised the expression she wore. There were tear tracks down each cheek; her eyes were tired, but I guessed it was that special kind of tiredness that comes with grief rather than lack of sleep. Though of course, the grieving brought that with it too. Her hair was platinum and her clothing the neat beige that belongs to upper class housewives and professional women alike, making it impossible to tell which one was which anymore. And with that thought something clicked.

'Josie, from the therapy group.'

She nodded and gave me a sad half-smile.

Freya had marched me to several group therapy sessions after Theo. She'd been allowed to come in with me, too, as moral support – and to make sure I actually attended. Josie had been a latecomer so we hadn't had much direct contact. But I thought we might have managed coffee once after my time at the group had finished. *Or did we only plan to?* I couldn't remember anything more then, other than she'd also lost–

'I'm here visiting Leonard.'

Her husband.

'It never gets easier, does it?' She nodded to the headstone.

What a hideous alibi my husband had become, I thought, as I wiped at my face to clear any mascara that was likely still clinging to my cheeks. 'No, no it doesn't seem to.' I managed a smile. 'But they tell me it does, so that's something to hold on to, isn't it?'

Again, she only managed a nod. She stepped forward then, though she was still on the pathway. She seemed to hesitate before speaking but soon managed, 'I hope I'm not overstepping, but your friend, from the group. Freya?'

The sound of her name sent a literal pain up my spine.

'She lost her son, didn't she?'

Another pain. I wondered whether my own nervous system were somehow turning against me; punishment for the unable mother. Because of course, I was only too keen to take the blame for the sins of my girl. *What did I do wrong?* Any mother in this situation must wonder. But what *had* I done wrong?

'I was just so sorry to hear about her loss. Will you… I mean, it might be strange, it's been such a long time and she and I didn't really… Anyway, will you please pass on my condolences? It's just a terrible…' She looked to be incapable of finishing a sentence and frankly I was glad of it. As far as I was concerned, she'd already said enough. 'You were close to him, weren't you? You must have been?' Then her eyes spread wide. 'Oh God, your own daughter…'

My first impossible thought was: *She knows*. And even though the ludicrous nature of that worry landed on me seconds later, I realised then, that that would forever be my thought now. If I didn't tell someone first, I would always be waiting for someone else to realise – for someone else to tell.

'Your daughter was best friends with him, wasn't she? Or have I… I'm imagining that, am I? Or…'

'No, no,' I leapt in then, largely because I couldn't stand to see the woman struggle any longer. 'They were best friends. Better than best friends, actually.' Tears filtered down my face again but at least I didn't have to worry about explaining them away. It was natural to be crying; I was grieving, again. But I suddenly felt as though I were grieving for my own daughter as much as I was for my best friend's son.

'Please, give my love to your daughter too? I'm sorry for

intruding on,' she nodded towards Theo's headstone, 'well, on your time together.'

I tried to smile. 'Not at all. It was good to see you, Josie, thank you for... Well, thank you for saying hello.'

'Any time. Perhaps I'll see you again.'

'I'm sure.' I turned back to Theo's headstone in the hope that it might extinguish the conversation, lest any other awkward stops or starts tumble from either of us. In my peripherals I saw her slowly walk away.

'Theo,' I rested my elbows on my knees and held my forehead in my palms, 'do I turn her in?' No sooner was the question said aloud and I clamped a hand over my mouth, shocked at my own disloyalty. But I wondered, too, whether that was the right word for it. I tried on others: sensible; moral; logical–

My phone hummed again and it was Jessica, again. But I wasn't ready; I never would be. That time, I hit the red button on the touch screen and sent her straight to voicemail. She wouldn't leave a message, I didn't think; she hadn't done all the other times she'd called. What would she say even? What was there she *could* say?

I traced the gold of Theo's headstone until I'd written out his name with my index finger. 'I'm so sorry, my love.' I wasn't entirely sure what I was apologising for, but still it had knocked against the back of my teeth, too keen to stay trapped in my mouth. And I felt better somehow for having said it.

I heard my phone shiver against the ground with another phone call and I sighed. I would have to go home to her. But when I reached to collect the handset I saw another name plastered there: Freya. *Oh God. I'm going to have to talk to Freya. I'm going to have to–*

'Freya?' I tried to keep my voice steady. My mouth was uncomfortably dry; post-gym dry, making her name sound odd.

There was a long pause before she said, 'My husband is cheating on me, Annie. My husband is...' The sentence disintegrated into tears and it took a second or two for her to clear the airway of her throat well enough to speak again. 'My husband is cheating on me, and my son is dead.'

I cried, hearty-heavy-weighted sobs down the phone line to her, then, all the while thinking: *And my daughter killed him.*

CHAPTER TWENTY-TWO

Kaleb had told her everything – including the part about me knowing. 'He told me that you'd told him to tell me,' she said and in my panic I worked to untangle the sentence. 'I'm not angry about that,' she added, and I sighed in relief. He told her he had feelings for this other woman, that it wasn't just an impulsive sexual thing, though she couldn't decide whether that made it better or worse. 'But then he said he doesn't want to leave me, he doesn't want for us to be over.' There was a long pause. 'I told him to get out all the same.' I didn't say anything; I only sat with Theo and listened to the outpouring and worked incredibly hard to keep my animal wails trapped in my mouth. I managed the occasional tut and huff, which felt like safe noises to be making. 'Are you home?' she asked eventually.

'No, I'm with Theo,' I managed.

'Oh, Annie, Annie, I'm sorry, I–'

'Wipe that word from your mouth,' I interrupted her. She was the only one out of the lot of us who didn't have anything to apologise for. 'I knew this was coming. I'm glad to be here for it.'

'Do you know,' she started and I thought there was a new wave of sadness in her voice, 'do you know that he was with her, the night that…' The sentence died in her mouth; we both knew how it ended. 'He told you that, didn't he? I think that's the only reason he told anyone. Because the bastard knew he was about to be caught out.'

I'd been sitting cross-legged for however long I'd been at the graveside and it dawned on me then, that my legs had gone numb from the position – or the panic. I fidgeted against the ground and put an extra inch between myself and Theo in the process. It brought it all back, hearing about Kaleb, and I could suddenly remember that bitter twinge-pull-push of disgust at realising the person you loved didn't love you enough – because of course, that's how it felt when someone betrayed you. And of course, that mention of betrayal only made me think of Jessica again.

'If he comes to you,' Freya cut my thoughts down their centre, 'if he comes to you, what will you…'

'I have no interest in backing Kaleb in this,' I answered. 'I will back you, all the way, including whatever decisions you might make about staying with him, or… Whatever alternatives you might be thinking of.' There were limitless options, of course; knowing Freya, revenge would be high on the list of priorities already. But that was Freya BR that I was thinking of: Before Ryan. Post-Ryan, losing her husband, too, might have been a grief too much to bear.

'I have to go,' she said with an abruptness then, as though she'd realised something. 'I have to go and shower and clean the house, and there's a client who I… I have to go.'

'Can the client not wait?' I asked, trying for a gentle tone.

She hesitated and then answered, 'I think I need it.'

I understood all too well the need for busyness. 'Do you want me to come over?' I offered and though it pained me, deeply, somewhere in the core of my belly, I felt a hideous hope that she would say–

'No, Annie, but thank you. I… I just need to be busy.'

'I'm here, when you need me.'

'I know.' I heard a smile in her voice, though I imagined it as a weak and tired one. 'I love you, Ann.'

'I love you, sweetheart. Go easy on my best friend, won't you?'

After we said our goodbyes, I checked the time – and cleared another missed call from Jessica – and then I leaned forward to kiss the headstone of my own cheating husband. Theo hadn't been emotionally attached to his indiscretion, and there had been advantages to that. Again, though, I remembered the roar-rumble-thunder of rage that had surged through me when he told me what had happened – and I thought back to that want, that burning need, to strike out, to throw things, to embrace whatever red riot of feeling was running through me.

'I still hadn't done it, Jess,' I said aloud as though she was there, before I turned back to the headstone and admitted, 'But Christ, there were times when I'd wanted to.'

I drove home thinking of Freya, and the loud betrayal I'd just inflicted without her knowing. I replayed the conversation, too, and queried my own normalcy through it all. By the time I was pulling up at home, I felt the deep burn of bile in the back of my throat and I forced myself to sit, breathe – *in through the nose, Annie, come on* – and try to steady myself for what was waiting beyond the door. Jessica hadn't tried to call again. I wondered whether she would have gone out, searched for me somewhere. But where would she have started? In moments of panic, I'd only ever gone to two places: to see Theo, or to see–

'Freya.' Her name fell out in a groan and I dropped my head back against my seat. 'Fucking hell, Freya, what am I going to do?' I tried to imagine what she might do; the only other mother I'd ever felt close to, besides my own – who wasn't there for me to ask. If her boy had killed my girl, would she shield him or would she turn him over? If I was honest with myself, I worried that I might hate her either way, and the thought of her feeling that way about me, about Jessica, turned over another wave of bile so violent that I thought it might break the sea wall of my throat. I opened the car door as a precaution, but short of a dry and painful retch there seemed to be nothing there, and I tried to remember when I'd last eaten.

I stumbled to the house like a drunk driver might on arriving home at the end of the evening, and struggled to manipulate the key, push, and lurch inside. I shut the door quietly behind me, as though trying to hide the fact that I was home. But when I stared down the green mile of the hallway, I could see Jessica was sitting at the kitchen table still, where I'd left her. She struck me like a loyal dog then, waiting for the return of an owner who had abandoned her.

I swallowed and took a deep breath before walking further. She was up and out of the seat, though, turning the tap, filling the kettle; trying to anticipate my needs, I guessed. Though what I needed was for her to tell me that it had all been some twisted lie. That, I thought, I could handle. I would take a delusional child over one capable of murder. *Manslaughter?* I wondered, and a high-pitched noise snuck out of me at the thought.

'I don't want tea.'

There was a long pause before she said, 'I think it's good for shock.'

'Don't be ridiculous, Jessica, that's just what people say when it's too early in the day for alcohol.' I went to the fridge and pulled out a fresh bottle of white. I didn't offer her any this time. I only took a glass from the draining board and then pulled out a chair at the table. It would never be too early for alcohol again, I thought, as I unscrewed the cap and poured a measure.

'I'm sorry, Mum.' Her voice cracked with tears. 'I'm so, God, I'm so, so...'

'Sit down,' I said, when I was sure she wasn't going to be able to finish her apology. 'I have questions.'

She followed instructions. Her sleeves were pulled down as far as her fingers and when she sat in front of me I could see that she was worrying at them; keeping her hands busy. My own hand was shaking as I lifted the glass to my mouth and I took three hungry swigs one after the other, as though drinking water after a run.

'You said you pushed him,' I started, but paused for another sip. That was the point where I'd stopped her – 'Just stop fucking speaking, Jessica.' – and stormed out of the house with my keys in hand. 'He hit his head, then what happened?'

'You know what happened,' she said, her voice unsteady.

'No, Jessica, I don't. Ryan was strangled.' I ducked my head to try to catch her eyeline and when she looked back at me the most dreadful mixture of love and disappointment overtook me. I wanted to hold her, kiss her forehead, tell her everything would be okay; which is to say, I wanted to lie to her, and make promises that I couldn't keep. *But isn't that what being a parent means?* I didn't know then, I didn't know what my parent responsibility was. So I only said again, 'He was strangled.'

'I...' She shook her head and I wondered what the end of the sentence might have been. 'I pushed him, and he fell, and hit his head. He was on the floor, then, and he was...' Another headshake. I needed her to start finishing things if I was ever going to understand; try to understand. So I waited a second longer. 'He was so out of it, but he was being so cruel, *so* cruel that I hardly even recognised him. And I crouched down, because I only wanted to check he was okay, and he... he just kept being cruel.'

'You can't kill someone because they're being cruel, Jessica.'

'I know that.' It was nearly a snap but then she checked her tone. 'I know.'

'How was he cruel?'

Tears were running down her cheeks and again I resisted the

urge to comfort her. It wouldn't help, I decided; I couldn't do anything that might let her think this was okay.

'He called me a crazy bitch. He said I was frigid, I wasn't... I wasn't, I don't know, I wasn't as good as this other girl, and that's why... He said he'd needed to see what he was missing and I...'

'You what?'

'I put my hand over his mouth to stop him.' Her hands were cradling her forehead then, her elbows on the table. We'd always told her it was rude to do that. But in the grand scheme of things, it hardly seemed worth reminding her. 'I put my hand over his mouth and he tried to push me away but he was so slow, and sluggish, and the drugs... I guess the drugs made him weaker or... I don't know. He didn't... he couldn't push me away, but when he tried I just pushed harder. And I had one hand on his mouth, and then my other...'

'You went for the jugular,' I said, my voice flat and rough around the edges. *You went for the jugular, like any scorned woman might have done.* And I thought again of her father, and the night he'd told me, and the many things that had been within grabbing distance for me to throw. *Only I didn't.* 'Is that how it happened?'

She nodded. There were tears dripping from her face onto the table and I watched them pool.

'And then you left him?'

'I didn't know what else to do.'

'You could have not killed him, Jessica!' It wasn't a statement; it was a shout. And the sound of my own anger surprised me as much as it did her. She stared up at me wide-eyed and open-mouthed and it was only then that I realised I was standing, looking down at her. My small, young girl. My girl, with her whole life ahead– 'Get out. I don't want to see you right now, Jess. Go upstairs.' I had to censor the sentimentality before it could get a hold of me. She followed instructions with a shaky nod and like a montage film reel I thought of all the times I'd reprimanded her in her short life. I longed for the over-indulgence in cookies when she was a child, for the missing ten-pound note, for the half an hour over her curfew. When her back was to me I added, 'You speak to no one. Don't even so much as answer a text message.'

It seemed unlikely that she'd confess to anyone else, I thought. But then it occurred to me, too, that only yesterday I'd thought it was unlikely she might commit murder. *Yet here we are...*

CHAPTER TWENTY-THREE

After Jessica had gone upstairs I spent too long staring into the darkness of the garden, as though a clear answer might step out from behind a shrub and wave its hands at me. But of course, nothing of the kind happened. Instead, I only saw the day change from dim-orange-peach peel through to absolute black. My legs ached from standing at the kitchen counter for quite so long, and I found that I was having to grip hard onto the edge of the work surface to guide myself around the room. I went upstairs soon after and tried to sleep; or rather, I hoped that I might have been tired enough to simply pass out. But there was no luck. I heard Jessica leave her room once after I'd gone into mine. There was the flush of a toilet, the creak of the stairs, the bang of a cupboard closing. I wondered whether she was looking for the wine. The last bottle was standing tall on my nightstand next to me then, though; not for an emergency thirst, but only to keep it from her. I couldn't trust her to drink anything anymore; I couldn't stop myself from imagining what might spill out from a loosened tongue. When I heard the creak of her coming back upstairs, shortly followed by the soft click of her bedroom door, I decided to give up on sleep. I took the wine and retreated to the living room. And I tried to remember as much as I could of what she'd told me.

I'm not expert enough to know for certain how it works. But I've heard it said before that the brain will block out trauma until a time when it's ready to deal with it. I could only remember snatches of the story; small details that made a mosaic of her mistake – as if mistake were a strong enough word for it. I wondered whether the full memories would ever come back, or whether I even wanted them to. Perhaps if I could block out the confession entirely, I could lower myself back into that world of not knowing.

Would that be better?

I moved about in the darkness and found myself back in the kitchen: the scene of the recounted crime. Though it had the crutches of comfort too. The far end of the kitchen table was still a scattered mess with my work materials. There was a different A4 pad for every project I was working on; a different colour of bright Post-it available for them all. I swilled wine around like a strong mouthwash and reached for a pad then, and I pulled free two sheets of paper from the back of the book. At the top of one I wrote CONS and on the other, PROS. And I spent a full two hours drafting, redrafting; crossing out and colouring in, the many reasons why I should-shouldn't-should turn my own daughter over to the police. *For having killed my best friend's son.* The thought chased its own tail around my head like a demented dog. After completing the PROS list I curled it into a tight ball and aimed for the general direction of the bin; I missed. Then I pulled free another sheet of paper and tried to remember everything I'd written down on the first version – how much of it I might be able to deliberately forget, to lessen the reasons.

'Of course you won't do this,' I said into the list; my elbows on the table and my head balanced between two unsteady hands.

The further down the list I scanned, the more I saw my handwriting deteriorate. I had scratched down, *Because it's the right thing to do* as many as four times, and crossed it out twice.

I grabbed at my phone and pulled up WhatsApp. Theo's phone was long disconnected, but his number still hovered there, complete with a suggestion that I invite him to join the service. In the especially lonely hours, I would draft messages only to delete them later. Now, though, I found my thumb lingering over the keypad of my phone before I realised there was nothing I could say. There were no imaginary conversations to be had. Instead, I tapped out: *Would you want to turn her in for this?* and underneath that, *Or would you want to protect her as well?*

There my decision stared back at me; there my real feelings were.

I blinked hard and sent two lonely tears running down my face. Then I back-clicked from the app, threw my phone down and went back to my lists. The space around me was so horror-film-silent that when the handset started to hum across the wooden surface of the table I flinched at the noise intrusion. I checked the wall clock before I even checked the caller: 2:37am. Freya.

I answered with a shaking hand and a breath so trapped in my throat that I thought it might stifle me before it could escape. She spoke before I had the chance to.

'You can't sleep either.' I didn't answer, only let a pause swell. 'I saw your WhatsApp was online.'

Bastard thing. 'It's a rough night here,' I said, and I could hear that roughness in my voice, which sounded like it hadn't been used in as long as a week. I wondered whether the shouting earlier had left it scratched and tired; which was an understated version of how everything else about me, inside me, felt by then too.

'Do you want to talk?'

I huffed a laugh. 'I'm pretty sure that should be my line.'

It felt like a physical pain to have Freya's kindness then. I decided that whatever happened, I would never feel deserving of that, ever again. And that replaced the pain with a sadness that only ached.

'Kaleb has been here all night.'

'Explaining himself?'

A noise like a grunt fell out of her. 'Trying to.' I waited a moment; it felt like there was more to come and then– 'How fucking dare he, Annie? How fucking dare he dip his wick elsewhere and then expect *me* to make everything better for him, to tell him that it's fine and we can work it out and– Our son has fucking *died,* Annie.' The same caught breath, or a new one, maybe, spread out its elbows and dug into the insides of my throat. I set a hand there and rubbed with my fingers but it didn't ease. 'Our boy is dead and my husband may as well be.'

It only took seconds for her to realise what she'd said.

'Oh fuck me, Annie, I'm so sorry, what a thing... Jesus, I'm–'

'Don't. Don't apologise for any of it. I'm here for it.' *And I deserve it...*

I stared down at the lists again and read them through twice while she berated Kaleb for his actions. He deserved her wrath, too, albeit in a different way to me. When she eventually paused for air and, I thought, a good glug of something in the background, I tentatively suggested, 'Do you want to make a list?'

She barked a laugh down the phone; an abrupt and harsh noise like an unexpected belch. 'Beautiful Annie, you are the only person I know who would suggest that at a time like this.'

'Sometimes they help.' *Sometimes they don't...* I thought, looking again at my own. 'It was just a thought.'

'I don't know that a list will help. He... I...'

I waited for the false starts to stop before I said, 'People do make mistakes.' Theo had said exactly that. It was months later, when I was trying – and at that time, failing – to move past the infidelity that had moved into our home like an angry squatter. 'People make mistakes and they learn, and they regret them.'

I realised then, in a horrible flicker, that I hadn't even paused to ask whether Jessica did. She had guilt, that much was apparent enough. But regret. *Is there any of that?* I wondered, and my stomach made a churn-grind-bubble as though answering for her.

'He didn't say he regrets it,' she answered.

But that doesn't mean he doesn't, does it? I didn't say it aloud. Largely because I knew it wouldn't help. But also because I knew that the question had nothing much at all to do with Kaleb and everything to do with my own fresh wave of worry.

'The police are coming over tomorrow.' The subject change wasn't exactly unwelcome. But the sheer mention of police sent an increased temperature creeping up me. By the time Freya expanded, I was sure there was a bead of sweat growing to become a damp patch of skin between my shoulder blades. 'They've said there are some updates, some new things they want to talk through. I… I don't even know what to expect. What I should be expecting at this point?' *It's still early days* was all I could think to say but what use was it? I couldn't placate her with that anymore; not knowing what I knew. 'Will you be here for it?'

The heatwave in my body grew to uncomfortable heights. I leaned on the table to support myself as I stood and then I crossed the room to the patio doors. They were already unlocked and I shoved them open with a force. She must have misread the pause as something else because she added, 'I don't want Kaleb here for it.'

The cool air was a comfort. I felt my breath become unsteady then, though, the kind of unsteady that sits as a precursor to vomiting. I remembered the feeling well from too many drinks with Freya, morning sickness, hearing my daughter confess to killing her boyfriend. The third entry in the list made it worse and I felt a small shudder move through me then, an earthquake starting in my gut.

'He...' I started but I let the sentence die. It was no use in reminding her. I wasn't going to be able to get out of what she'd asked of me. *I'll never be able to get out of any of this*. 'Of course I'll be there.'

'Thank you, Annie. I... I can't do this on my own.' I wanted to tell her that I knew how she felt. Though of course, I hoped I would *never* know how she felt; I wouldn't have wished it on any parent. 'They said they'd be here at around lunchtime. I don't know what that means really.'

I hesitated. 'I'll come over at twelve, thereabouts, just in case.'

'Thank you,' she parroted. I could hear the tiredness creeping in around the edges of her voice by then.

'You should try to sleep, sweetheart.'

She sighed into the speaker. 'When I wake up, I remember it all.'

I looked down the length of the garden and breathed in another mouthful of bitter air. 'I know, lovely Freya, but you still need to rest.'

'Will you?'

'I will if you will.'

She laughed. It was a pact we'd made during pregnancy and carried through our friendship. I'll try the pump if you'll try the pump; I'll have another drink if you'll have another drink; I'll get a side order if you're having one. 'I'll try,' she said then. 'Thank you for being there, here, Ann.'

I turned inward to face the mess of papers across the kitchen table. 'Where else would I be?' The papers were separated down the tabletop; one side for work, the other side for working out the moral grey area of harbouring my own daughter. It was a before and after portrait of Ryan's death; it belonged in a gallery. 'Try to rest, and I'll be there tomorrow.' I hesitated before I added, 'I love the bones of you, Freya.'

'I love you.'

When we finished the call I went back to the drawing board but left the doors wide open. The PROS and CONS lists were exhausted. So instead I pulled free a fresh sheet and I wrote *Girl from the party*. Underneath, I added *Kaleb's bit on the side*. Then I spent a full hour writing down the names of everyone who might have wanted to hurt Ryan; anyone who I could think to blame.

CHAPTER TWENTY-FOUR

Jessica was trying to be quiet, but she still woke me. I must have fallen asleep somewhere between the sheets of paper. And I wondered whether she'd thought to glance at them on her way past me. I quickly collected them into a pile before I even looked at her. But when I glimpsed up I felt a new wave of horror; I wondered how many more of these influxes there could be. She was wearing her school uniform. Her hair was scraped back into a high ponytail but it didn't hide the grease creeping in at the roots. She hadn't bothered with make-up either, and her tiredness was writ large over her pimpled skin; she always had a breakout whenever she was stressed. *Is that regret?* I wondered and I opened my mouth as though I might ask. But instead a different question emerged.

'What do you think you're doing?'

She jumped and turned, a white slice of bread in hand. 'I'm making toast. I…' She glanced around but I didn't know what she was looking for. 'I was making breakfast, before school. I… Did you want tea? I didn't want to fill the kettle in case the water woke you. I'm sorry.'

'You can't go to school.'

'I can't sit at home,' she said to the floor.

'For now you can. You have the perfect excuse,' I snapped, then corrected the comment. 'You have the perfect reason.'

She opened her mouth as though to answer but only shook her head instead.

'What?'

'Mum,' whatever was coming was hard for her, I could see, and I steeled myself for it, 'do you hate me?'

And from that single question, everything else fell away. I pushed back from the table and rushed across to her and grabbed her in the tightest hold I could manage. I squeezed her close and felt her body relax into mine as though she were letting me take her weight, and seconds later, I felt the judder of tears. Her shoulders shook gently as she fought to keep the feeling in but with every 'Shh' and every 'Come on, my darling girl' I felt her lean into the outpouring, too, and soon she was sobbing like a child with a grazed knee and a broken bicycle. And I thought, *This is regret. Thank God, this is regret.*

'I could never hate you, Jessie, never.' And despite all this mess, I knew that much was true. Then, like every good parent must do at one time or another during their child's life, I comforted her with a lie. 'I'm going to fix this. I'm going to find a way to fix all of this.'

The innards of the house looked like Freya's creative brain had exploded. Hardly any time had passed since my last visit, but somehow there were slick lines of paint now patchworked through the hallway. She was an expectant mother trying out colours for the baby's nursery. *Or tomb,* I thought though I tried to shake that idea away. The stripped wallpaper had been cleared up and the photographs removed entirely and I wondered whether they would be replaced when the walls were painted in a single colour – or whether Freya's grief and anger would see her take Polyfilla to the small entry wounds where nails had once been hammered in. I don't know what face I made when I stepped into the space, but it at least made Freya laugh.

'I know the place is a state.'

'It's…' I searched for the right word. 'Different.' She laughed again, and then trod straight into the living room. I followed and saw there was already tea set out and waiting. 'In all the years I've known you, I have never once seen you use a teapot on any occasion.'

She murmured a weak noise. 'I might have started something like a renovation in the loft. There's so much shit up there. This,' she gestured to the tea set, 'I'm pretty sure it must have been Mum's, or Nan's even. I can't think why else I would have kept it. Whatever, I thought I'd try it on for size.' She landed hard on the sofa. 'Does it suit me?'

Nothing about this suited her. Freya looked exhausted. *No,* I corrected the word, *not exhausted*. Freya looked as though she'd been punched in the nose, sending a ripple of purple out beneath each eye. It was clear she'd been crying, too, and I wondered whether it was husband or son – or both. I deliberately sat on the sofa opposite, rather than taking the seat next to her, because I thought the proximity might help. But when I stared across the room to assess the damage of her, I realised that now I, like Jessica, couldn't stand to meet her eyeline. Shame washed over me like a river breaking its banks and I felt another sweep of temperature, the same from the night before. *I can't live with this,* I thought then, and soon after, I remembered the PROS – how they far outweighed the CONS.

'How's Jess doing?' she asked as she leaned forward to pour tea.

That, at least, I could give an honest answer to. 'She's a mess.' But I couldn't say any more. So instead I opted for deflection. 'Have you heard any more from Kaleb?'

'That cheating fucker,' she nudged a teacup and saucer across the table in my direction, 'he needs to stay away from here if he knows what's good for him.'

'Do you know…' I started, but a thick lump formed in my throat and I wondered what the word was for the feeling that comes before guilt; when you can pre-empt feeling like a terrible human being. *Forgive me, Father, for what I haven't done yet. But decided in the dead of night that I must.* 'Do you know who the woman is, did he say…?'

She shook her head. 'I don't know the specifics.'

And then I dropped it; the small grenade that I hoped might hit a target. 'Do you know whether Ryan knew?'

Her eyes narrowed at the question. She left her own teacup untouched, dropped back into the sofa, and cradled her forehead. Her eyes were closed and she looked as though she were thinking, hard. 'Christ, I hadn't even…'

I was glad when the doorbell sounded then, for fear that whatever conversation that span out might be too much to bear. My stomach was already an anxious animal but at least I could busy myself with welcoming the guests into the house. 'You stay there, sweetheart, I'll get it.' And when I was safe in the wild of the hallway I took two deep breaths before reaching for the handle. 'Freya is just through here,' I greeted them. They were the same detectives from before. But Haynes looked surprised to see me. Shaw shot her a glance before stepping into the house ahead of her. And all I could think was, *They know.*

Freya had only said that the police had an update. And in the dead of the night before I'd decided that if – if-if-if – I was going to protect my daughter then I needed to know everything that I could about what was happening behind the scenes. If they suspected Jessica – if-if-if – then they wouldn't want me here, though, of course; they wouldn't have anything to say if-if-if–

'Freya, thanks for letting us come over today,' Haynes said, and when I chased the detectives into the room I saw they'd taken my safe distance seat. I made a point of sliding my teacup over, and then I positioned myself alongside my friend. I didn't like that they could see my face.

Freya let out a huff-laugh-sigh. 'I'm hanging on your every word. I'll never say no.'

I looked up in time to catch Haynes glance at me, then back to Freya. She flashed a downturned type of smile, her lips pulling at each corner. 'Of course. We do have some news for you today, though, which is a step in the right direction for the investigation.' I felt as though someone had snuck their fingers in through my belly button and plucked my intestines like a set of guitar strings; a rumble emerged that everyone pretended to ignore. I had to hope that it sounded like hunger rather than guilt. 'Kaleb isn't here?'

Freya narrowed her eyes at the question. 'No.'

Shaw lowered his head and stared into his lap, as though ready to take any beatings that might be forthcoming – for the good of his fellow man. But instead, Haynes only nodded her understanding. Of course they knew why Kaleb couldn't be there; he'd told them before he'd had guts enough to tell anyone else.

'Annie,' my head shot up at the sound of my name in Haynes' mouth, 'this is actually news that might concern you, too, or Jessica, more specifically. I know that her and Ryan were involved.'

'In love,' Freya corrected her, and I envied her that belief. Ryan had clearly followed in his father's footsteps when it came to his understanding of how to love someone. But I said nothing and allowed her that blissful ignorance. I did not know Ryan had cheated; Jessica did not know Ryan had cheated. I reminded myself on a loop, and I readied my expression for the kind of shock the police might be expecting in response to any announcement they were about to make.

'They were in a relationship,' I added, 'yes. Jessica is... Jessica is how you'd expect a grieving girlfriend to be,' I said, answering a question that they hadn't yet asked. I felt the pressure of Freya's palm gripped around my thigh, then, in a supportive squeeze, and I reached for her hand.

'How was their relationship, do either of you know?'

Freya clasped her fingers into a tighter grip. 'They were happy as far as I'm aware. Ann?'

I murmured in agreement. 'Besotted.' I forced a laugh. 'It was always quite sickening to be around them, wasn't it?' I turned to catch Freya smiling. 'I'm not aware of any problems they were having, no. Sorry,' I shook my head gently to feign confusion, 'why are you…'

'We've recently had some results come back from the forensics team, the pathology team.' Haynes became more flustered with every word, and I noted that Shaw wasn't in a rush to help her. The nerves I was forcing, feigning, suddenly became much more real. *What hasn't Jessica told me?* 'Is there any reason to believe that Ryan and Jessica might have had some kind of open relationship?'

'What?' Freya and I snapped in unison. I wasn't sure which one of us had the greater right to play the outraged parent, so I lowered back in my seat to at least give her the chance.

'Why the bloody hell would they be–'

'It isn't an accusation,' Haynes interrupted, her palms upheld. 'It's just a line of enquiry that we need to consider before…' *Before what?* She seemed to be waiting for one of us to throw some light on the evidence she hadn't disclosed yet, and like any mother, coiled to protect her young, I felt too ready to spring in defence. 'Ryan tested positive for Chlamydia, Freya.'

The announcement burst into the space of the living room like a green smog. Much like the seconds that follow a distinct blast, the noise hummed somewhere deep inside my ear cavities and I found that I was straining to hear anything else Haynes might be saying but I couldn't see her lips moving. I could only re-hear the blast, re-hear...

'Which of course means–'

'Jessica might have it too,' I said, finishing her sentence. There had been no need to feign anything. I was sure my shock must look as real as it felt.

'Did your daughter give my son...' Freya snatched her hand away.

'Now, Freya.' Haynes was poised to stand then, and I wondered what sort of outburst she was expecting. But I knew Freya better than that. If she was going to reach for the jugular then she would only ever do it with–

'Has Jessica been tarting it around? Is that what you're telling me here?'

I tried to keep my voice steady as I asked, 'Does cheating run in the family?'

I saw Haynes and Shaw swap a glance. Neither of them looked ready to interrupt then, not when the real shots had been fired. And from the stunned expression on Freya's face I guessed that she was suffering the impact of this second blast – and in her own living room too. I was sorry for the comment, truly. But when it comes to mothers protecting their young...

'We'll need for Jessica to get tested, Annie. Is that going to be... Will she...'

'No, of course she won't be comfortable with it,' I barked. 'But she'll do it all the same.'

'As a matter of urgency, if that's at all...'

Haynes appeared to have lost the ability to finish a sentence. I shot her a hooded look and nodded. Of course it was a matter of urgency; my daughter could be sick with something that the boy she murdered gave her. Each separate part of the realisation knocked into the next and I found myself lurching forwards, my arms pressed against my knees, and my stomach pulsing.

'I'm sorry, I need a minute.'

I rushed free into the hallway, where the air was still clean, and pressed my back against the cool of the wall.

'I'm sorry, Freya, I know this is a difficult thing to hear,' Haynes said.

'That's all people seem able to say to me at the moment.' Her voice was tired and cracked with feeling. 'That's all I keep hearing from anyone, difficult things.' My knees buckled under my weight and I lowered myself to a crouch before they had the chance to give out beneath me. 'I just can't believe it. I'm sorry, I can't. Not of either of them,' I heard the tears start to come, then, 'I can't believe it of either of them.'

I pressed a hand hard over my mouth to catch my own sob before it could escape.

CHAPTER TWENTY-FIVE

The waiting room was olive. And when I say the waiting room, I mean every part of the waiting room. The walls and floor were seamless with each other, the ground only distinguishable by what looked like small glitter flecks that broke up the blandness of the colour scheme. The chairs, NHS-issued, had seen too many rears in their short lives and I tried not to imagine the various diseases, warts and all that had been pressed up against them. We had booked an appointment in advance – to the top of the list on account of Haynes having thrown her name around – but somehow we were still waiting. Initially, the detective had asked whether Jessica and I would see the police's own medic for the tests to be done, but Jessica's look of physical pain at the mere suggestion had rooted us to a quick no for that option. It said something of her discomfort, that she'd rather sit inside a sexual health clinic than a police station, but there was nothing about this that couldn't be passed off as grief, shock, or another entirely natural reaction to circumstance. That's what I was telling myself then; it was the only way to keep in the vicinity of calm. Or the new calm, as I considered it, that came with sleepless nights, nervous tics, and heart palpitations. Given that that was what was rattling around inside my own innards by then, I couldn't imagine how this all must feel for Jess.

I had tried not to ask antagonising questions. But her baseline response to everything was so deadpan, so disconnected from it all, I started to wonder whether antagonising her mightn't be a bad idea – at least I would know my daughter was still there somewhere, inside the shell that looked like her. She had reacted poorly to the news – of course she had – but since, everything had looked like an autopilot setting for her. Even while sitting in the waiting room, scanning the posters that brandished details and statistics for every venereal disease under the sun.

I reached across to grab her hand. 'Are you okay?'

She only nodded. I bit back on the question that I really wanted to ask. The million dollar, deal-breaking question that would make the floor fall through if she answered incorrectly. *Did you already know this was a possibility?* I'd thought it several times over but what use was there in knowing? I decided several times over too. She already had motive. She already *was* guilty.

'Are you okay?' she asked then, and my head snapped around. She wasn't looking at me, only staring into the abyss of Chlamydia cases on the wall opposite her. I followed her glare and wondered whether she was reading about the woman who now couldn't have children, or the man who'd lost his girlfriend to a stupid mistake. The latter option seemed more likely. Jess had never been interested in children. 'You must be so disappointed in me, Mum,' she added, when I didn't answer soon enough. I wanted to drop to my knees in front of her.

'Sweetheart,' I tugged gently at her hand until she turned to look at me, 'did you cheat on Ryan?' She looked confused. Her forehead ruffled and her face made something like a grimace. It was the most animated I'd seen her in two days. 'Then what on earth is there for me to be disappointed about?'

She looked ready to answer but instead of anything verbal, she only shot me a look. Such a telling look, too, that I knew what she would say, if she had the words for it; if we were safe in the jail cell of home. *Of course,* I nodded, *of course there's something for me to be disappointed in you for.* 'I'm not disappointed about this,' I added, then dropped back in my seat and matched her stare. '*This* isn't your fault.'

I'd only ever been inside a sexual health clinic twice in my life – and both times, I had been the Jessica. *No,* I remembered, *that's not quite fair.* The first time I'd been supporting the Jessica of the situation. She was a friend from university; one that came complete with a careless boyfriend who had found 'something' that he was worried about. I never found out what the something was, but whatever it was, she didn't have it. And we seldom ever saw that boyfriend lurking around her halls of residence again for the semester that followed. Then, there was the time I really was the Jessica. After Theo told me about the woman – the woman who he *hadn't* used protection with – I told him he needed to get screened, and without even waiting for his results, I decided that I would too. These things, I realised then, these tests, there's a large element of trust involved in giving someone the opportunity to physically hurt you like that. While I was still reeling from the emotional hurt of the cheating, I wouldn't have trusted Theo with so much as a funfair goldfish. By the time our respective test results had arrived I'd threatened to throw him out as many as four times.

'What happens, if I've got it?' she asked, and I was grateful to be snapped out of the memory. 'If it comes back that he...'

'They'll give you antibiotics and it will go away.'

'Just like that?'

I squeezed her hand. 'Just like any other infection.'

'Have you ever...'

I understood the question, of course. 'No, I haven't.' I saw her sag in the seat next to me, and I thought what a strange thing it was to be disappointed by. So, following suit with a set bar of behaviour that I was becoming overfamiliar with by then, I lied.

'But there have been quite a few times when I thought I might have got caught short, I can tell you that much.'

Her face cracked into a smile; a loud-burst reaction that seemed to catch her off-guard as much as it did me. 'Christ, what a fucking horrific thing to feel reassured by.' She rubbed at her forehead with her free hand, and in that motion her face fell back to its default blank. 'Sorry for swearing.'

I laughed. 'I think that's probably allowed in this situation.'

There was a long and weighty pause before she asked, 'How's Freya?'

Freya was furious – with everything in the world. In the days since the police visit we'd spent time together, though, and she had decided that both of us should reserve judgement on our potentially cheating children until we had more information to work with. I had said nothing, and only agreed with the lie of my own cheating child for the sake of letting Freya have that benefit of the doubt about her own. The last thing she needed in the aftermath of Kaleb – whose behaviour had now escalated to turning up on Freya's doorstep and shouting things like, 'I'm grieving, too!' – was to know that her son was a cheat as well. Besides which, Jessica's test – positive or negative – wouldn't prove one way or the other whether Ryan was the cheat. I knew that much. It would only prove whether our kids were safe enough to have been having protected sex. It turned out they were – so I hadn't failed in *every* area.

During Kaleb's last visit I'd been the one to answer the door. 'She has to talk to me,' he'd said and I'd answered plainly, 'No, she doesn't.' Even though I knew that that wasn't true. To find a precarious middle-ground in it all, though, I'd offered to talk to him instead. We were going to meet, though we hadn't made set plans to. I wouldn't do it without Freya's approval, I'd decided, but I'd also decided there was information inside Kaleb's head that might become useful – like how trustworthy his mistress was, and how sturdy her alibi. I swallowed hard then, and heard the gulp echo up from my throat. I hated this methodical thinking, this constant looking for loopholes that had become daily life. *But what are the other options?* I thought then, not in my voice but in Theo's. In all my imaginings, I had managed to make my dead husband complicit in this plan to shield our daughter. I had to believe he would have been.

'She's worried for you, sweetheart,' I answered, because I was sure Freya must have expressed that at some point. During one of many conversations where her head had been resting in her palms, or pressed against the kitchen table, or lying in my lap, she must have. 'But she isn't angry, or disappointed. She's just... confused.'

'Would one of them cheat?' Freya had asked; I could remember that much. Then, 'Do you honestly think Jessie would cheat?'

At the time I thought how telling it was, that she'd asked that of Jessica and not Ryan. Though that may well have been a side effect of the lying husband.

'Jessica–'

'Yes?' she snapped before the nurse had even got to her surname.

'I'm sorry, lovely,' the woman crouched in front of my daughter, 'we're running a little bit behind on the usual clinic today but we will get to your appointment, okay?' She squeezed my daughter's knee and smiled. 'Sit tight.'

'Like there's another option,' I muttered as she moved away, then instantly regretted it. I had always hated those people who made it hard for others to do their jobs, yet I could slowly feel myself becoming one of them. 'Do you want a drink or anything, sweetheart? I can go and grab something?'

'No, Mum, I'm fine. I...'

The sentence died on her lips when the door in front of her opened wide to eject a young woman; I guessed she must be Jessica's age. She had brilliant red hair that was scraped back into a tight bun, and make-up that I thought had probably been perfect at the start of her appointment. Now, though, it was running in tracks down her cheeks; a deep black that scored her pale complexion. She had her jumper pulled down to cover her hands, but in one of them there was hanging a nondescript white paper bag, with a box of something peering over the top. Her eyes were downcast but something made her look up on her way out, and that's when she spotted us – more specifically, she spotted Jess. The redhead let out a sad laugh and veered her direction slightly, to head more in ours.

'Makes sense that I'd see you here.' Her opener seemed hostile but it didn't match altogether with her voice, which only sounded sad. 'Have you been in yet?'

I turned in time for Jess's confused answer. 'No, I… Not yet… Why does it make sense?'

The girl waved the bag about and the paper crackled in the movement. 'Ryan.'

'Oh.' Jessica pushed herself back into her seat, as though she might be able to apply pressure enough to crack through the chair, the wall, back out into the open air of the car park somewhere beyond the building. 'Oh God.'

'Jess,' the other girl started to answer but then shook her head. There was an empty seat alongside Jessica that the girl dropped into, but she angled herself in a way to keep a look on my daughter too. 'I'm really sorry, Jess, but Ryan, he wasn't who you thought he was. He… Ryan had a lot to get out of his system.' She waved the bag again and nearly, but not quite, managed a laugh. 'Literally, it turns out.'

Jess stayed stock-still and stared into the ground. She looked as though she'd been hollowed.

'I'm sorry,' I took up the opportunity to speak, 'you're here because of Ryan?'

The redhead looked startled then, as though it had only just occurred to her that a parent was within earshot. The friendly demeanour soon turned to embarrassment and she was quick to stand, and step back from us.

'I'm sorry, I...' She moved away and I resisted the urge to reach out and grab her.

'*Are* you here because of Ryan?' I pushed.

Embarrassment shifted to shame. She clutched the bag with both hands and worried at the open edges of it. Then she managed a nod. 'There's a few of us who will be.' And though she could no longer bring herself to look directly at my daughter, she added, 'I'm so sorry, Jess.'

That was the tipping point that sent Jessica fleeing. She pushed past the girl and made instead for the disabled toilet that was four doors down the wide corridor. I said nothing else to the redhead and only followed Jessica's lead. Outside the locked door, I listened to the quiet sobs and retching that came from within. And I tried not to feel too guilty for the part of me already imagining the ways in which the suspect pool for Ryan's death might be about to break open.

CHAPTER TWENTY-SIX

If anyone had walked in, they would have assumed I was deep in the throes of a new work project. The kitchen table was again covered with clusters of paper – some stretched out and scribbled over; some balled up like small projectiles – brilliant pink and yellow Post-it notes, highlighters, even. The only thing that gave my frantic thinking away was the empty wine glass – and the bottle standing tall alongside it. I was drinking it like an athlete might drink water but, paradoxically, it was the only thing that helped to declutter the thinking that I'd brought home with me from Freya's earlier in the evening.

The police had been in touch with her to say they were liaising with the school about Ryan's infection. I could see the distaste on her face as she tried to explain that; the near-physical pain in the quiet admission that her boy, and her husband alike, had managed to trick her into believing they were something they weren't. Somehow, even without Jessica's results – that we were all still anxiously waiting for, two days in – Freya had settled into the thought that it must have been Ryan who cheated. I hadn't even had to lay the seed.

'Look at Jessica, look at how she's being,' she'd said, her head balanced in a palm and her stare angled at some unspecific point on the living-room wall. 'It's grief that girl is going through, not guilt.'

I didn't correct her – and I felt my self-loathing bloom another petal.

'Did they say when her results...'

I nodded. 'Seventy-two hours.'

'Is she showing any...'

I shook my head. *No symptoms.* I knew the worry without hearing it.

She'd told me, then, that there had been phone calls from two mothers at the school. They hadn't gone to the police, but instead straight to Freya. One was a girl who'd tested positive and I wondered whether it had been the pretty one that Jessica and I had seen at the clinic. One had, to my surprise, been a boy; a cuckolded one, apparently, and I guessed it was someone that girl had been involved with. Or worse still – a thought I had but didn't share – there were other girls who had spread it to other boys, and so on, and so...

'I'm going to have to call the police and tell them tomorrow.' She collapsed forward and rested her head on her knees. 'Jesus, who was he?'

Being close to Freya was becoming increasingly difficult. But in that moment, a primal best friend instinct had kicked in, and I found myself dropping to my knees in front of her. I shushed and rubbed and lifted her head to face me.

'He was your boy.' My voice cracked. 'He was your boy and he was lovely and...' I forced out a half-laugh that managed to trigger the first flow of tears too. 'He was your boy and he was a bit stupid and he got things wrong. And...' Then came more tears. 'And he didn't deserve what happened to him.'

Saying the words aloud nearly killed me, too, especially given that I truly, in my mother's heart, believed them. About as much as I believed my daughter didn't deserve to have her life ruined over it all, either...

When I'd arrived home earlier in the evening Jess was already asleep. I'd stood in her open doorway and watched her, like I'd done a hundred times before throughout her life. Only this time, instead of the peaceful sleep of a toddler, child, early teen, it was the tortured sleep of a– *criminal.* I hoped the thought might autocorrect but it didn't. Because of course, that's what she was now. And I'd carried that thought through the walls of the house, a house full of memories of my beautiful girl growing up – and I knew then, that my options were limited to one thing now.

That's when the kitchen table exploded. There were scribbles of names – girls, mothers who I knew who had girls at Jess's school, even if I didn't know them by name, other schools in the local enough area – and there were things highlighted and there were times noted down. I looked every bit the archetypal detective from a cheap made-for-television movie – right down to the alcohol that I swigged at regular intervals. I had tried to go without it. But the hard stare of the plans I was making was too much to bear, even if I was doing it for the right reasons.

'The wrong thing done for the right reasons is still wrong, Jessica.' I remembered the reprimand that Theo had given our daughter when she'd thumped a boy at school because she'd seen him thump someone else. Jessica had been made out as the bully, and I'd defended her to my back teeth. But Theo had taken a more realistic approach. 'You can't just go around laying into people, whatever you think they've done wrong.'

I sighed. 'We did everything right, Theo. We did *everything* right.'

And I would keep doing everything right – even if it was wrong.

I took a worryingly large glug of wine straight from the bottle and tried to ignore it as a warning sign. When the burn in my throat had stopped, I rushed up to Jessica's room again, pounding on the stairs like a herd of something loud and angry, though I tried to quell that emotion. She was already half-awake when I walked into the room and I thought my thundering must have stirred her. Still, I shook her the rest of the way to be awake and she soon shot upright and looked around her room in a childlike panic, as though expecting to see something wrong or out of place there.

'Mum, what– Did something happen?'

'I need you to come downstairs.'

'Are you drunk?' She spat the question, seemingly outraged by the prospect.

'Probably. But I still need for you to come downstairs.' I left then, without waiting for any further questioning from her. Out of the two of us, I decided I had a greater right to be the inquisitor. I lingered at the top of the stairs to make sure she was up and moving, and when I heard that she was I trod my way back to the kitchen. I was sitting at the table again by the time she came in.

She paused stock-still in the doorway when she saw everything laid out. 'Mum... Have you even slept?'

'No, I've been working.' I gestured to the papers. 'Clearly.' The alcohol was giving me a hard edge that I was only noticing now; now that I had to communicate directly with the culprit. But perhaps that hard edge was what I needed to get through. 'Can you sit?'

Jessica followed instructions. She was pulling her wild hair into an equally messy ponytail, and trying to read my scruffy notes too. 'What is...'

'This is everything I know about what Freya knows, and it's everything I know about what you know. But there are some things I don't know.'

She opened her mouth, her bottom lipping bobbing up, down again, up– 'What do you want to know?'

I nearly laughed. 'I *want* to know nothing. I need to know what happened to the clothes you were wearing the night Ryan died.'

I'd never been able to say it in such a blunt phrase before. But I knew that doing away with sentiment was the only way. That, and booze, I thought as I topped up my empty glass and took a generous sip.

Jessica looked ashamed then, and I felt a turn in my stomach; pre-nerves at whatever was coming. 'They're in a bag in the bottom drawer of my wardrobe.'

The wine helped to grease a cog and a horrid memory turned over. 'Is that where you've been hiding booze too?' Jessica nodded with clear reluctance. I remembered back to the night Freya and Kaleb had been here for dinner. Freya had found wine in the bottom of Jess's wardrobe then, which must mean she'd also found– 'Christ Almighty.' I pulled a sheet of paper towards me and made a note of her answer in the corner of it. 'And the phone?'

'What–'

'The phone you texted him from. The fake phone, whatever you call it.'

'I told Sally that I lost it.'

An uncomfortable beat of silence passed between us. She even managed to hold eye contact then, too, but I couldn't decide whether that newly discovered confidence in her was a good thing or a bad one.

'That isn't what I asked.'

'It's in my sock drawer. But it's broken.'

'It's broken, or you broke it?'

'Both.'

'How did you break it?'

'Mum–'

'Good God, Jessica!' I slammed my palm flat against the table and the impact made us both jump. 'Just answer my bloody questions.'

The confidence in her dropped. 'I soaked it in bath water. Then I stepped on it. Then I put it in the drawer. The SIM card is snapped. The phone won't turn on.'

I wrote down everything as she said it. 'Is there anything else you've covered up, any other evidence from that night? Any way, at all, that someone can place you at that party?'

She thought for a second. 'Not that I can think of.'

There was only one question left to ask then, and it was the deal-breaker in all of this. I'd gone back and forth on whether I could speak it aloud, and it took another two mouthfuls of wine and a wince before I could steady myself enough to ask. Still, I had to avoid her gaze as I said it. 'Was it an accident?'

She looked confused, then hurt. I thought I saw a flicker of anger, too, a near outburst of something. But it settled back into what looked like pain, and it broke my fractured heart to know I was the cause of it. But I had to know too. I *had* to. Because if it wasn't, because if there was *any* chance that something like this might happen again, then–

'Yes. It was...' She petered out and took an audible gulp.

I felt my whole body sag with a strange kind of relief. I hadn't quite realised until then how much I worried she might say it hadn't been an accident at all, and I hated myself with a violent passion for feeling that way. But if it hadn't been an accident, if it hadn't been a one-time hideous mistake, then I knew it would change everything.

'I wish... I wish it had been me, Mum. I wish it had been me instead. Then he could still be here, and everything would be okay.'

I clenched my eyes closed and thought of Theo; the phone call; the blue lights. *Nothing would be okay.* I pushed my chair back with a loud squeal of wood against floor tile and rushed over to her. She was crying by then, too, a shoulder shudder of tears that she was trying to hold in, but when I stood and wrapped my arms around her from behind I felt her relax into the sob, and I cooed her and stroked her hair and craned around to kiss her forehead.

'Everything is going to be okay now, sweetheart.' I rocked her gently. 'Everything is going to be okay. I have this plan…'

CHAPTER TWENTY-SEVEN

By the time Kaleb arrived two days later, the kitchen was a shadow of its messy self. After the talk with Jessica I'd slept for ten hours straight and woken up with a sore head and a surprising clarity. There was something restorative about having made a decision; Theo always said that I was better when I had a plan. Even though the plan meant that my morals had been balled into an uneven mess and discarded somewhere; I thought I felt them hardening in the base of my gut, releasing small and strangled cramping sounds that were hard to ignore. But still, I tried. Fresh from sleep, I'd sent Jessica to school and then set about cleaning the kitchen from top to bottom. I bleached every corner until the room stank of crime-scene cover-up; an all too apt comparison. Then I'd called Kaleb and asked if we could talk. There was a noticeable relief in him and an immediate, 'Yes, please.' In the interim between me arranging that and him arriving, I'd also told Freya what my plan was. Not the whole plan, of course; no one could ever, would ever know that. Not even Jessica, yet.

'I think it's worth knowing more about the woman he's involved with,' I'd told Freya – over the phone, because I didn't know whether I could hold a neutral enough expression for the lies that were ready to tumble out.

'Why?' Her tone had been hard-edged; if we'd been in person, she might have cut me with it. But before I even had the chance to explain she said, 'Oh my God,' as though she'd realised. 'Won't the police have… I mean, surely the police…'

'I'm sure they have,' I'd agreed with her, gently. 'But I was thinking about it in the early hours and I can't get my head around this unknown, Freya, and…' I took a hearty swallow. 'And if this hadn't happened with Ryan, you would have asked him everything by now. You would have sat the bastard down and quizzed him start to finish.' I didn't need for her to agree; I was best friend enough to know. 'I'm obviously not suggesting you do that. But let me? Because we're grappling around for answers, lovely Freya, and there's a whole pot of them waiting on Kaleb.'

There was a long pause before she said, 'You're a good friend, Annie.'

No, I'm not, I thought, *I'm a fucking dreadful one.* But I was at least trying to be a good mother.

When I opened the door to Kaleb I could see straight away how nervous he was. He shuffled awkwardly and let out a tentative huff that was nearly a laugh, but then his expression dropped into something plain. 'Annie, I…'

'I know.' I didn't want to make this harder for him, even though a large and angry part of me thought that I should. But that wasn't what this was for. 'You'd better come in.' I stepped aside and made space for him in the hallway. He lingered there like an unfamiliar guest. He was no longer the Kaleb who'd been in the house a hundred times or more before. He was a stranger now. And though he didn't realise it, I was a stranger by then too. 'You can go straight into the kitchen, if you want, the kettle's not long boiled.'

There were fresh cinnamon rolls plated in the centre of the table. I'd baked them first thing that morning, before Jessica was even awake and readying herself for school. It was out of character, anyone would know, but I'd needed something to keep idle hands moving.

'You shouldn't have,' Kaleb said when he saw them.

'I didn't,' I snapped back. 'Jess needed something to keep her busy.' What was one more lie? Besides which, in comparison to the other bear traps I was laying, this one hardly felt like an untruth worth feeling guilty over. 'You're welcome to one, if you want. Tea?'

'Please.' He took a seat without waiting for a formal invite, and somehow I was simultaneously pleased and pissed to see him drop the guest-in-someone's-home demeanour in favour of a more comfortable one. Part of me was desperate for his discomfort. He stared at the rolls but didn't take one. 'How is she?'

I span around from my spot by the worktop. 'Which one of them?'

'Can we start with Jessica?'

Exhausted, guilty, desperate. 'She's about as good as you'd expect her to be. I sent her back to school yesterday. She needs… I don't know, she needs something normal, I think. I hope.' Though of course, normalcy had nothing at all to do with why I'd sent her back to school. What Jessica needed was to get close to people; she needed an ear to the ground; she needed to be complicit. I went back to making the tea. 'We'll try it for a couple of days and see how she gets along. I can't push her if she isn't ready, but still…'

'You're right. She needs something to keep her going. Is she still applying–'

'Don't try to make this normal.' I filled two cups with water and watched the teabags bob for a second before I went to get milk. 'Nothing about this is normal and I think we're both well aware of it.'

Kaleb stayed silent then, until I crossed the room with our

drinks.

'I appreciate you seeing me,' he said when I sat opposite.

'I'm seeing you for Freya.'

He pulled in a greedy amount of air. 'How is she?'

'How do you think she is?' I stared straight at him and openly dared him to hold eye contact with me. He managed it for three seconds – I actually counted, a measure that helped me in holding my own nerve – and then he fixed his eyes on his drink. 'Her son is dead and her husband was screwing someone else at the exact time it was happening. It's a wonder she hasn't fallen off the fucking ledge with it all.'

'Annie, don't–'

'Don't you dare tell me not to be angry.' Theo had done that too. And I parroted back the exact same expression that I could remember saying to him. 'I think you'll find that every woman in the fucking world has a right to be angry.'

'She won't see me. Fucking hell,' he cradled his head, 'the police won't even see me. Everything I hear from them, I hear through phone calls. They're visiting the house to talk to Freya but she won't even let me be there and… fuck!' He dropped his hands back to his drink, and I wondered whether he'd throw it. I had broken three wine glasses in the last five days. But I shouldn't have judged him by my own standards. After all, I still had a child to fight for. Meanwhile, Kaleb only looked defeated. And despite my anger and my best-friend scorn, I found that I was reaching across to grab at one of his hands then.

Your daughter murdered his son, I reminded myself. The thought was an intrusive one. I had it too often now. Like that urge to jump that comes with standing on a bridge. You know you won't do anything about it. But still, it's there, lingering somewhere at the back of the brain. What would happen if I jumped. What would happen if I told him that– Kaleb squeezed my hand and pulled me out of the idea.

'You said on the phone that you've got questions. Meaning…'

'Freya has questions.'

'It's all out there now, you can ask what you like. The police already know the sordid fucking details of it.'

'Is it anyone Freya knows?' That had been Freya's first wonder; had she been betrayed by someone she knew? *Yes*, I'd thought immediately then, *but not in the way that you think*. 'She's worried that–'

'It isn't anyone either of you know. I met her at a work thing.'

'Conference?' I asked, and he nodded. 'How long?'

He pulled his hand away. Whatever answer was coming, I knew I wasn't going to like it. 'Twelve months.'

'Christ, Kaleb.'

'I know, all right, Annie? I... I already know how bad this is.'

'Why did you... I mean, what possessed you?'

He shook his head and narrowed his glare into his tea as though the leaves might have an answer. 'I don't even know how it started, what brought us together. She... She started talking to me, at airport security of all places. They were trying to take make-up off her, and she joked with me how petty it was. There was nothing to it. Christ,' he rubbed at his forehead then threw his arm out in a wide gesture, 'she could have spoken to anyone. It was just chance that she spoke to me.'

'And then what happened?'

He shrugged. 'We bumped into each other at the conference. Again, there was nothing to it. We were in totally separate rooms, seminars, the lot. We literally just said hello on our travels.' He paused to sip his tea. 'I honest to God thought nothing more of her until the flight home.'

'And then what, you felt like you'd missed an opportunity?' I couldn't keep the spite out of my voice, even though I saw how much it winded him.

'And then she was on the same flight again.' He shook his head and rubbed hard at his eyes. 'I know it's terrible, Annie. I know I'm a middle-aged cliché and all the rest of it but fucking hell, do you know when the universe is sending you a sign?' I arched an eyebrow; I couldn't help it. 'Okay, maybe you don't know. But sometimes, Annie, let me tell you, it *feels* like the universe is flinging you a great fucking sign, and when I saw her at the airport I… I just said hello, and then everything span out and got bigger and…'

'Did Ryan know?'

With his head hung low, as though the shame of it were a physical weight around him, he nodded. 'He only found out recently.'

Is that what made him think he could go out and cheat on my daughter? I wondered. Kaleb must know by now what Ryan had done. Still, I swallowed the urge to mention it. 'And? What was his reaction?'

'He wanted to tell Freya. He was… he'd been threatening to tell Freya.'

'The woman, did *she* want you to tell Freya?'

'No,' he answered too quickly. I imagined them having long and winding conversations about it. Isn't that what married men do with women they'll sleep with but won't leave their wives for? Or maybe that was what I'd been coached to believe. 'She didn't want Freya to find out, at all.'

'Is she married too?'

'No, she just… She never wanted it to be that, neither of us did.' A heavy sigh chased the words out. 'Christ knows what we did want it to be.'

'So Ryan knew, and the woman, she knew that Ryan knew?' I waited for his murmur of confirmation. 'But she didn't want Freya to find out, which also means she didn't want Ryan to open his mouth?'

His head shot up. 'She was with me the night that it happened.'

'I didn't ask.'

'You didn't need to, Annie, I know what you're implying. The police implied it, too, for a minute. But she isn't a murderer. Christ,' he pushed back from the table, 'is that what this is all about?'

'Am I asking you about a woman that I don't know a thing about who happens to have a solid motive for murdering your son? Yeah, I guess I am, Kaleb,' I said, matching his outrage. But inside I was basking in a morbid glee that I hadn't been the first to float the idea. 'Maybe I am being unfair, maybe she didn't do it. But I've got a best friend in pieces over this and I won't leave a stone unturned, I can tell you that much.' I had practised the lie. It came out angrier than it had when I'd been alone in the bathroom, but still, it had the desired effect. Kaleb sank low in his seat as though suffering from a slow puncture.

'She wouldn't, Annie. It's... it's ridiculous to even think it.'

'Maybe so. But people do ridiculous things when keeping a secret, don't they?'

Of course, I didn't need an answer. I was becoming living proof...

CHAPTER TWENTY-EIGHT

Jessica sat opposite me at the kitchen table, quietly crying. Her eyes were low-running taps; single streams steadily pouring and occasionally landing on the wood table beneath her. I reached over to grab for her hand but she ignored the gesture. Her mobile phone occupied the tabletop space between us. The light of it had died out from a lack of touch. But beneath the dead screen there was the text message we'd been waiting for. The call had come shortly before it; DS Haynes, letting her know the result. Somehow, though, receiving the text message only minutes later had made it worse; the hard edges of each word had cut through her, I guessed, the black and white of it; the undeniable reality that–

'Of course he didn't get it from me.' She huffed a laugh, a sad and defeated noise. 'How could he possibly have got it from me…' Her tone was so downbeat that I wondered whether she'd been hoping, in some perverse way, that perhaps he had; perhaps the test would be positive and perhaps that would mean he hadn't strayed. I could see the watercolour logic despite the impossibility of it – and I felt a stab of sadness for her. I wanted to say something reassuring, something that would ease the lacerations of the news. What was there though?

Aren't you glad you did it now? A spiteful voice chimed once, twice, three times, and I wondered what twisted self-defence mechanism of my own must have kicked in for the question to have even crossed my mind. Though it was chased around by an idea that felt just as spiteful: *If it's crossed my mind, has it crossed hers too?*

The shock-sting-vibration of my own phone ringing made me fidget in my seat. I pulled it free from my front pocket and saw Freya's name.

'You should answer,' Jessica said, without my even saying who was calling. 'They've probably called to tell her as well.'

'Jess, I want to be here for–'

'You should answer.' She snatched her phone from in front of her and stood up at such a speed that the chair rocked unsteadily behind her. 'I'm going to school.'

'Jess, wait–'

'Talk to Freya,' she shouted back, and punctuated the comment with a slam of the front door.

I was tired, so tired, of talking to Freya – another thought that I hated admitting to. But still, I swallowed a deep mouthful of air and hit the green button on my phone screen. 'Sweetheart, how are you?'

'They've told her?'

I sighed. 'This morning. Just now, actually.'

There was a long pause before she said, 'Annie, I'm so sorry.'

'Good God, Freya, what for?'

'My son. For what my son... for what he did to your daughter.'

The sentence was a buckle tightening around my neck. *I'm sorry for what my daughter did to your son...*

'Do you want to come over?' I said instead. 'Jess has just left for school.'

'She's brave, that girl is.'

She was following instructions, that's what she was doing. Though of course, I couldn't admit such a thing; I added it to the pile of unruly truths that I would never be able to part with. Instead I only murmured in agreement and said again, 'You're welcome to come over, if you want, Frey. I doubt there'll be much work done here today, and I'd be glad of the company.' I stopped there, for fear of laying it on too thick. The low silence – filled only with the sniff of early tears down the phone – started to get the better of me though. 'I tell you what, I'm going to pop the kettle on now. The front door is open. So is the offer.'

'Thank you, Ann,' she answered in a strangled tone, then disconnected the call.

I was almost disappointed when the front door squealed open ten minutes later; though disappointed probably isn't the right word. I listed near synonyms like a grounding exercise as I waited for Freya to tread down the hallway to me – where I was already making two strong cups of tea. She came to a stop close behind me while I faced the counter still, and made her arms a vice around my waist. It crossed my mind that she might squeeze the life out of me. I stopped what I was doing and set my hands over hers and let her hold me like that for a second.

'The police are going back through his phone records. Calling every girl in his recents, calling every girl he might have texted.' I thought of the anonymous number that Jessica had used. The phone was in pieces at the bottom of a landfill dump now – I'd trashed it days before – and the SIM card long gone too. 'I'm so embarrassed for him, Ann.'

I turned to face her with a cup of tea in each hand. 'Come on, it's strong.'

She laughed. 'I think I need something stronger than that.'

'Well,' I looked at my watch, 'we should probably wait until after twelve.'

'You always were the sensible thinker,' she said as she took the drink. It felt less like a compliment and more like a curse, but I managed a smile. 'I think I need to call the school.'

'About what?' I led her into the living room. I was tired of big conversations and kitchen tables and confessions. I dropped into my armchair instead and pulled my legs up beneath me. Freya landed hard, defeated, on the sofa opposite me.

'The...' She shook her head. 'What the police have found, about the tests.'

I tried to think, think faster, but I couldn't see how this did or didn't fit with the plan that Jessica and I were living out. 'I don't see how the school can help, sweetheart. What are you...'

She rounded her lips and forced out a long breath. 'They might be better placed than the police to hear about other cases. Do you think?'

It crossed my mind that she might have a point. 'Are you thinking about the girls on his phone? Girls he might have been... involved with?' I asked in a tone I hoped was soft, and she nodded. 'I don't know that school will find out faster than the police, sweetheart.'

She ran a hand through her hair. 'I can't be doing nothing, Annie. I can't.'

If the police were ringing through girls then there was every chance they'd find the one we were looking for eventually; before Jess might manage to, even. But if the school systems were looking for cases, too... I tried to do the fast maths: Three searches were better than two.

'Do you want to call the counsellor?'

Her head shot up. 'Do you think that's the best route?' I saw a spark of life in her again at the thought of doing something, trying something. And my own motivations twisted themselves into a Gordian knot, mangled up with the deep-seated need to help a friend – though of course, I'd never be able to do that, not really. So instead I only nodded and forced a thin smile, to which Freya answered, 'I'll get my phone.'

Deborah Day picked up on the fourth ring and I wondered whether she'd got Freya's number saved. I imagined the school counsellor steeling herself before answering the call. 'Freya, how are you?' Then there came a sharp intake of breath. 'I'm sorry, that's a stupid question.'

Freya and I were side by side on the sofa by then, and I felt her thigh tense at the question. Her mobile phone was on loudspeaker, balanced on her leg. I held her hand through the labour of having a conversation.

'Mrs Day–'

'Deborah, please,' the counsellor interrupted, and I felt Freya's irritation come off her in jagged cartoon waves.

'Deborah, I was hoping to talk to you about Ryan again.' Her voice cracked over his name and I wondered whether she'd ever be able to say it again without that same stab of pain. 'I have some questions and… well, they're more thoughts, really, I suppose, I…' I gave her another squeeze. 'I have Annie here, too, just so you know,' she added in a hurry.

'Morning, Deborah.'

'Annie, how's Je…' My daughter's name died out on her lips though; another stupid question. 'I hope you and Jessica are taking good care of yourselves,' she said instead, and I took some comfort from the implication that that must mean Jessica hadn't been to visit her recently. *Or is that wishful thinking?* I worried that too much prodding from anyone now might cause all sorts of things to come spilling from my daughter's mouth, as though she were a confessional piñata at a murder mystery party. But still, I had had to send her out into the world if our plan was going to– 'You said you wanted to talk about Ryan?' Day pulled me out of the thought before I could tumble too far into the rabbit hole of it.

'Have you heard,' Freya took a deep swallow, 'have you heard about his problem… the problem they found during the… when they were investigating.' Freya shook her head and closed her eyes. This, at least, was one thing I didn't have to claim guilt or responsibility for; though there was a ferocious wave of guilt that soon came from the fact I was taking comfort in this moment at all.

Day hesitated before she answered. 'Yes.'

Freya and I both waited for more but nothing came. I resented Day, then, for making my friend work so hard for what was already a difficult conversation. I opened my mouth to intervene but Freya did the same, and instead of the grief-stricken friend she'd been moments ago, she was a hard-edged thing instead.

'Mrs Day,' she said pointedly, the name brittle enough to lacerate, 'you're obviously aware that my son contracted a sexual infection some time before his death. The thing we know now is that Jessica doesn't have it. But it stands to reason that other students might. Do you know anything at all about that?'

This was the old Freya; the Freya before the death of a son and the loss of a loyal husband. But as soon as she'd ejected the words, she shrank in the seat next to me. I heard her breathing become rough in her chest as though the air were catching against something en route through her, and I thought I felt the beginnings of a tremor in her close body too.

There came another hesitation. 'I really wish I could help you but–'

'But you're choosing not to,' I spat. Freya's frustrations had leaked into me. Our motivations were much the same, even if our reasoning was different: we both wanted someone to blame for Ryan's death. 'Mrs Day,' I squeezed Freya's knee, 'you're obviously aware that these are more than extenuating circumstances and all we're asking is that–'

'Annie, Freya,' I wondered whether this was the tone she took with the students, 'I'm really not at liberty to discuss the health concerns of our pupils.' What little air there was left in Freya escaped out of her in a sigh and she leaned forward in a near-recovery position. I caught the phone before it dropped from her leg and cradled it in an open palm. 'But off the record,' and at that Freya was upright, 'I can tell you that the police have been here, to investigate the matter, and I believe they're doing the same at other schools.'

'Thank you, Mrs Day,' Freya managed. 'Truly, thank you.'

There were more lukewarm sentiments after that, before the call eventually ended.

I had never wished ill health on anyone before. But in those moments, I hoped to God they might find traces of the infection everywhere. Anywhere. Any new suspect would do.

CHAPTER TWENTY-NINE

Another week passed with nothing. Jessica and I fell into a cycle of silent scrolling. She would arrive home from school; I would fix her a plain, early dinner; we would sit in front of the laptop like it were a family television screen and stare through lists of teenage girls who were connected with her newfound friends at school. She was bonding with girls who had known, sooner than we had – in one way or another – that Ryan wasn't all he seemed to be. I didn't know how many of them had slept with him, and I didn't know whether Jessica did either. I wasn't sure I wanted to. But now, bonding in the only way teenagers knew how, they were slowly connecting to each other via social media channels – and we needed to use that.

When Jessica's stomach was growling with ill-feeling, after an hour, thirty minutes, sometimes as little as five, I'd say we could stop, and still she persisted for several minutes longer each time. Though tears would inevitably follow, I would have to find a soft enough voice to send her up to bed with a hug and a hot chocolate like she was still a young girl. When I watched her plod along the hallway each night, round the corner of the stairs, I found myself desperately wishing it were the case.

Meanwhile, in that same week, Freya and I found our own routine. She was trying to get on with daily life – a new tactic she was adopting, to varying degrees of success. She was placing twice daily phone calls to the police still, and ignoring thrice daily phone calls from Kaleb, who persisted in calling morning, lunchtime and night, even though Freya – and, on four occasions me, too – said she had no interest in talking to him: not about the affair, not about Ryan. Freya now knew that Ryan had recently discovered the affair, and that only added a new strain to her suffering. In every day that we spent together I felt the push-pull-shove of my emotional insides, and sometimes my literal ones, too – though I was attributing that, in part, to my dietary shift from three meals a day through to half a bottle of wine and two slices of toast, swallowed in a hurry when I'd sent Jessica to bed. But still, when Freya and I were together, I tried for outward normality. I tended to any need – cup of tea? No problem. A work break? No issue at all. Harbouring your son's murderer? I've got you covered – and while we both tried to shift closer towards clearing our backlog of respective workloads, we alternated whose house we spent time in. After Monday to Friday on this, though, I needed the freedom of a wide open space – somewhere I wouldn't have to hold eye contact or conversation with her. The thought bulldozed my guts but I couldn't get away from it; guilt was a monster and it was eating at the linings of me.

'Why don't we go for a walk?' I asked over the edge of my laptop, and Freya's face wrinkled at the suggestion. 'We don't have to go far but, I don't know about you,' I slammed the lid closed, 'I could really do with a change in perspective.'

She almost laughed. 'You bloody writer types.'

'I know, we're very tortured.' I clambered up from the floor of her living room, where I had spent most of the morning sprawled with briefs galore and little to no incentive to work on any of them. 'Get your coat.'

Despite the vicious temperature drop that looked to have happened overnight, the sun was still shining. Freya and I walked side by side through dead leaves, bare trees and dog-walkers – all of whom insisted on saying 'Hello' or 'Lovely day, isn't it?' whenever we passed by. We took it in turns to respond to them, a system we'd quietly agreed to that saved us both the hassle of consistent politeness. We were nearly through the wooded areas and out the other side, onto the main high street, when Freya finally spoke to me directly.

'They're not going to find who did it, Annie.'

No, they're not. I swallowed bile and said, 'You don't know that.' That was true, too; she didn't know. All I knew was that I was doing my damnedest to make sure they didn't find out anything that would lead them back to Jess. 'The police still aren't making headway?' Whenever I asked this now – which I did, often – it felt less like an innocent query and more like I was scouting her out for insider information. And while I hated myself for that, it was only one thing in a growing list of reasons that caused me to lay awake at night and wonder whether I'd get a front-row seat in purgatory, or whether worse still, I'd be relegated to the back of a theatre, forever doomed to peer over the heads of those criminals and degenerates in front of me, but never quite see a show for myself. There were some nights when I wondered whether *this* was already purgatory: the dead husband; the murderous daughter; the fact that I would never, *ever*, be able to look my own best friend straight in the eye again without the churning urge to confess that came with it. But the worst thoughts were inside the imaginary hellscape theatre I'd made: Would I ever see Theo again? And is Jess down here with me?

'They've arranged for tests to be rolled out across the year group which is the most embarrassing thing I've heard in my life to date. But they've said that's only one lead and there are other possibilities they need to explore too.'

'Nothing about what they are?'

She didn't answer though, and my head snapped up – in time to catch her shaking hers. 'Sorry, no. Nothing about what they are.' She dug her hands deep into her pockets and hunched her shoulders higher, as though she were about to plough through a snowstorm rather than an early winter's afternoon. 'The woman, the one Kaleb…' We hadn't given her a name; it felt like a horrible political statement to leave her so blank. She had only been The Other Woman whenever we spoke of her. 'Do you think they've talked to her?'

I'd told Freya about my talk with Kaleb, and the gaping black hole in The Other Woman's alibi; the question of what she did after Kaleb had left her. And I knew, too, that Freya had taken it upon herself to pass that information along to DS Haynes.

'They must have done.'

'They fucking better have done,' she snapped. The old Freya again. She was in there, deep down, resting on her haunches and sharpening her teeth. I wondered what exit wounds Kaleb might be wearing now if Freya had found out about the affair under other circumstances; whether there would still be a murder investigation happening, albeit of a very different kind.

The area was built up around us by then and we were dodging other pedestrians as we talked. Freya had done a fine job of avoiding anyone who might talk to her about Ryan. She couldn't stand the sympathy, she said; worse still, she couldn't stand the judgement. I knew that an indoor coffee somewhere would be out of bounds for that reason but, in a bid to change the subject, I suggested a middle ground.

'Shall we get something to take back with us?' From the corner of my eye I saw her glance up at me. 'We could get a hot chocolate from somewhere. Or better still, it's about that time of year when all the coffees we don't understand the names for suddenly have cinnamon and/or pumpkin spice added in front of them, what about one of those?'

She huffed a laugh. 'That would be nice, Ann, thank you. Why don't we…' She came to a stop and I followed. Her eyes were darting between shopfronts behind me. But seconds in, they widened, then narrowed, then– 'I don't fucking believe this.'

Freya shoved past me with a force and charged to something out of sight. I span around to follow her, darted between the crowds and couples that were bunched between one side of the high street and the other. I was trailing behind her by a few steps but I could see where her glance had landed: a posh coffee shop, where her husband was sitting in the window seat, with company.

'Freya, Freya,' I shouted, 'come on, you don't even know that it's her.'

'Of course it's her,' she yelled back without turning.

And of course, she was right. That, or Kaleb was out for an overpriced lunch with another woman – who he was holding hands with across the table. When I saw that I, too, felt a wave of fury and suddenly felt less inclined to halt the charge of the woman scorned. Instead, everything in me wanted to offer to hold her handbag for her while she took the first swing. It was the most normal I'd felt in days.

'Nothing going on anymore, huh?'

Freya was towering over them at the table. I was two steps behind, ready to divert any waiting staff or an offended manager who might try to break up the scene.

'Frey,' Kaleb was up and out of his seat, 'Frey, listen to me.'

'Don't you fucking Frey me, you lying piece of–'

'There are children here,' someone cut her off and I turned.

'Then cover their ears.'

The woman glared at me then cast an eye to the drama unfolding behind me – where Freya was still shouting. Some silent understanding passed between the two of us then, as though she'd just realised what was playing out. 'Cover your ears, love, it's grown-up stuff,' she said to the child sitting across from her, who immediately followed the instruction. The woman went back to her salad.

'Freya, nothing *is* going on, we were just talking and–'

'And holding hands,' Freya interrupted. 'And sharing lunch. And...'

The Other Woman coughed and raised a hand. I couldn't see Freya's expression then, but I knew too well the death-stare she might have shot her. Still, she only lowered her hand and in a too-soft voice said, 'He's right, there really is nothing going on. It's just lunch.' She had the cheek to sound casual about it too. 'It's just some comfort, after–'

'You dare say his name.'

I lunged forward in time to catch Freya by the shoulders. 'She isn't worth it.' I turned my friend away from the table and stared hard at a dumbstruck Kaleb. 'Neither of them are.'

Freya broke free of my grip and aimed for the door.

'Annie,' Kaleb started, but I raised a finger to pause him.

'Don't. Don't talk to me, don't try and appeal to my better nature. You fucked up, Kaleb, and now you're fucking up again.' I looked between them. 'Don't call me, don't call Freya. You're on your own.'

I rushed from the bustling café and started to chase down the high street in the direction that Freya had fled. The fury in me was violent red and growling. And this, I thought, was the best best-friend thing I'd been able to do for her in weeks.

CHAPTER THIRTY

I heard the front door slam and Jessica's bag land heavy in the hallway. 'I'm just finishing up some work,' I shouted through from the living room. I'd had an open fire burning for most of the day, using joggers, a hoodie, gloves for kindling. What had started out as the stench of singed clothing – burnt now, to only a few remaining scraps – had become just a faint whiff. The kitchen, somehow, held too much bad energy at the start of the day for me to work in there; though the living room was a corrupt space now too. Still, there had been too many late nights hunched over that kitchen table, putting together clues that didn't belong with each other and lines of enquiry the police hadn't got to yet. There were too many tense and ugly conversations with Jessica there already too; ones that had seeped into the wood grain and stained the panelling. I'd needed the change of space so instead I'd brought everything work-related into a fresh room and commandeered the coffee table, where I was awkwardly hunched up with my laptop. It was the first day I hadn't worked with Freya, either, while she was visiting her parents up north. She'd be gone for two days, she said, maybe longer; I thought she probably needed the change of a physical space.

I was quietly aware of Jessica lingering in the doorway, wordless. And when I looked up I realised there must have been a fresh wave of something. She was pale-faced and her cheeks looked to have collapsed somehow, sinking in against the outlines of her teeth.

'Sweetheart, what's–'

'I found out who the girl is.' She didn't need to add more but still she repeated, embellished, 'I found out who the girl is, from the party.'

The air rushed out of me in a sick relief. Jessica and I had been running our own private investigation into Ryan – and this, I thought, must be the first sordid break in the case. But from the look on her face, Jessica's own reaction was anything but the relief that I felt.

'Sweetheart,' I struggled up from the floor to greet her, 'sweetheart, sit down before you tumble down.' I guided her to the sofa. But once seated, she slid onto the floor instead and landed with her legs at awkward angles. She reminded me too much of a dead thing then. I clambered down to the floor to sit next to her and wrapped an arm around her shoulders. 'What happened? Did you... I mean, was it through the social media? Like we...' *Planned*. I couldn't bring myself to finish the sentence, though of course she would know its end.

She shook her head, then began to glance around the scatter of papers on the floor as though only just registering they were there. 'Why are you working in here?'

'I'm tired of the kitchen.'

She murmured, and I thought I heard some understanding there. 'I'm sorry, I've interrupted you.' Her voice was deadpan, and I began to wonder whether this was another wave of shock shifting through her. I clutched her to me and went to speak but she beat me to it. 'I should go.'

'Sweetheart,' I was pulling her to me, restraining her from fleeing, 'sweetheart, what you should do is tell me what happened. Can you try that for me?'

'Sally,' she answered.

'Sally knows the girl?'

'No, Sally heard girls at school talking.'

'About the girl from the party?'

'Mm. She and I were in the common room together but they didn't know we were there and... They were talking about Ryan. Everyone is always talking about Ryan.' She rubbed hard at her temples then, and scrunched her eyes closed. Her voice gave way, too, no longer flat and monotonal; instead, there was a ripple of exhaustion. 'They mentioned a girl's name that I didn't recognise but it's happening so much, Mum, so much.' Then came another break in her voice; this time one that I recognised as too much feeling for a girl her age to bear. 'There are so many girls that people are saying he was with, or involved with, and it can't be true, can it?' She turned to face me and I saw the bulbs of tears forming. 'He can't have been with *all* of them, how is that even possible?'

I kissed her forehead. 'I'm sure he wasn't, sweetheart.' Though of course, I wasn't sure of anything by then. I wasn't sure of Ryan, who he was, what he'd been doing. The only thing I felt occasionally sure of was that it was perhaps a good thing that my daughter had got to him before I had done. If this had all come out while he was still alive... *I would have killed him myself.*

'They were mentioning this girl over and over. Then they said something about hearing the police hadn't spoken to her yet, then they mentioned the party and...' Her stamina limped away and carried the conclusion with it. I hated forcing her to relay it all but–

'Sweetheart, I need to know what was said.'

'Sally and I had stopped talking to listen. One of them, it

might have been Bev, I don't know, one of them said something about the night of the party. That's when Sally leapt in.' She huffed a noise and it took a moment for me to realise that it was a feeble attempt at a laugh. 'She bolted upright like she was in a comedy sketch, making some big reveal or another. "What about the night of the party?" she said, "What is it that the police don't know?" And the girls all went quiet and Sall, she just stood there, ovaries the size of watermelons, hands on her hips and waiting.'

'She's a good friend, Sally is.'

'Christ, isn't she.' She pulled her knees up towards her and rested her forearms on them, freeing herself from my hug. 'The girl's name is Zoe Hallows. The police,' she turned to me, 'they're looking at kids from other schools, right?'

I nodded. 'They're looking into STI cases from other schools, that's what Freya told me.'

'That's why they haven't found her. She's a first-year university student.' She faced away and dropped her head between her knees, and her whole body shook with the sob. 'Christ, no wonder he liked her. She must have been better than me in every fucking way.'

'Jessie, no.' She pulled away sharply when I touched her back but I pulled harder until she collapsed with her head against my chest, sobbing like she would have once done when a nurse administered a booster. 'She isn't better than you, she won't have been better than you. Ryan was just…' I didn't want to say it, but the word knocked so hard against the inside of my mouth that I worried I might chip a tooth if I didn't let it break out. 'Ryan was weak. He was a weak, stupid boy with too good a face on him, and he took what he could get and I'm sorry, sweetheart, so bloody sorry that he took from you how he did.'

Jessica's body shuddered-juddered-heaved with feeling. I felt her tears soak through the cotton of my blouse. There was nothing I could say in those moments, nothing that would ease the feeling of her heart fragmenting off. So I only let her feel it all and cry it all out until minutes later, the exhaustion of the outburst set in. Her breathing became steadier and tears ran dry. Still, she clung to me, with her arms wrapped around my middle. I kissed the crown of her head.

'Sweetheart, I know this is horrible and it's hurting. But it's a good thing that we've found her. We've been *trying* to find her, remember?' She tensed so tightly that I thought she might have been holding her breath. 'This is part of the plan, sweetheart, and it'll be easier now–'

'Mum.' She shot upright and stared into me with a narrowed look. 'Mum, what the fuck? I… I can't… What is wrong with you?'

'With *me*?'

'With *you*, yes! Christ, you can't seriously be thinking of going through with this plan?'

'Jess, why the bloody hell wouldn't we? We've found her now.' This had been my bright idea: to find the girl from the party. Regardless of Jessica's feelings about her – Zoe, as we could now christen her – and Ryan, there was motive there. And that's exactly what we needed. 'The whole point of looking for her was so we could–'

'Frame her.' She spat the accusation. For a second, she looked truly repulsed.

'We're not framing her, Jess, we're just making sure the police have somewhere else to look. Christ,' I tried to grab at her hands, 'this is all to protect *you*, remember that, won't you? We're diverting attention, we're creating a bloody security net in case they find–'

'Me,' she cut across. 'And what about if they find something on *her*? What about *her* life?'

'Jessica, what about yours?'

The question seemed to confuse her. Again, she narrowed her eyes, but this time at a fixed point on the floor. I imagined answers-worries-thoughts knocking together in her head like a possessed Newton's cradle; one idea unable to run to completion before cracking into the tail of another. Soon, she shook her head and sent them all fleeing at once though, and instead said, 'I'm not ruining two lives for what happened to Ryan.'

'You're right, you're not. I'm not letting you ruin your own.' The answer rolled off me like the entire scheme was nothing to me and for the briefest of seconds I wondered whether my daughter was right; whether there was something wrong. But no, I was doing what any mother would to protect their child, and that's exactly what I told myself in the early hours of every morning while I was staring into the dark abyss of the garden cradling a cold coffee. *Every parent would do this* on repeat like a dawn affirmation that would get me through the day – and so far, it had.

'Jesus Christ, Mum, why not? I'm a murderer.' The word made me wince and she saw, but the reaction only seemed to spur her on. '*Murderer*,' she said as she struggled to her feet. She pointed at her chest to underscore the accusation, tapped hard at her sternum and said again, 'Murderer.'

'Jessica–'

'What would Dad say? What would Dad say right now, if he could see what you're doing, what you're becoming?'

It was the wounding shot. The hard edges of the words slipped into me and punctured each lung, and I found that my breathing came in sharp and ragged bursts then, as though teetering on a panic attack myself. After weeks of keeping it together, I thought, this would be the moment that undid me. But instead of showing any mercy – like I had done when she was stealing wine, refusing food, upchucking into the small hours with her mangled grief and guilt close at hand – my incapacity only seemed to spur her on.

'He'd be as disgusted with you as he would be with me.' And then she stomped from the room, every bit the petulant child.

She left me clutching at my chest as though the words had gathered there; a physical bunching that made it harder still to breathe. But it didn't matter to me. We had a plan, I reminded myself, we had a plan and I would see it through. *Because every parent would do this...*

CHAPTER THIRTY-ONE

Sunrises were coming later and later. I drove through the night and a spectrum of colours before I hit the limits of our own city again. Jessica would be getting herself ready for school, and I wondered whether she'd notice that my car was already missing – worse still, whether she'd worry, or even care. In the days since the argument we'd hardly spoken, and it crossed my mind that she might be grateful for my absence while she scuttled around the house and collected her things for the day. She might text me eventually – though of course, she might not bother too. By the time I was closing in on home territory, and turning into Freya's road, the world had fully yawned awake. Jessica would be walking to school by now, or on the bus if she'd run late. And at Freya's, Kaleb's car was already waiting outside the house. But the closer I came to it, the more I could make out the dark silhouette of him sitting in the front seat still; waiting for me, I guessed. I had agreed to sit in on their necessary discussion, but I'd been looking forward to it in the same way that one looks forward to a smear: it will be embarrassing, uncomfortable, but highly necessary and, long-term, everyone would be the better for it. During the night-time drive, I had worked through the many ways in which this conversation might run. It was a sequence that had eventually collapsed into thoughts of what Freya might throw – both in an accusatory sense, and in the sense of anything that wasn't bolted down might become fair game.

I parked just along the road from him, and by the time I'd unbuckled he was lingering at my car boot. He looked every bit the sheepish young boy – but caught with his hand in another woman's knickers. I felt a roll of something unpleasant move through me and I tried to swallow it back before it could bubble up and out of my mouth. I had promised to be impartial – or at least, impartial enough.

'Thanks for doing this, Ann.'

'Make no mistake,' I clicked my car locked, 'I will always do anything to support Freya, whatever that involves.'

He smiled. 'I understand that.'

'But,' I moved closer and lowered my voice, 'I really don't give a shit about you. So if you're expecting anyone in that house to be on your side, don't.'

A rush of air escaped him. 'Understood. And very deserved.'

I powered along the garden path leading to the front door, which was now painted in a royal blue. It was the latest in a long line of distraction techniques that Freya had been trying to busy herself with. From behind me I heard Kaleb's hesitant footsteps, then we both came to a stop – he some steps behind me still – while we waited for Freya. I didn't know what we could expect to find behind the front door. But I certainly hadn't been banking on the old Freya answering: her hair was in loose curls and a half-up-half-down style; her make-up was well-touched up, with enough foundation beneath the eyes to hide where her tears would normally collect; and she wore a brilliant red lipstick that made her look as though she'd just taken the jugular out of something – it also happened to be a colour we both knew Kaleb hated women to wear. I smirked and cocked an eyebrow in approval, and when I kissed her cheek hello I whispered a low, 'Good girl,' into her ear.

'Kaleb,' she said, when I was safely inside the house. She stepped aside and gestured. 'You're allowed over the threshold. I'm not sure there's an adage about cheating husbands.'

'Frey, thank you, I–'

'I've set up the dining room for us,' she interrupted him before, I guessed, anything like an apology could spill out. 'There's tea already in there, for anyone who wants it. Annie, have you had breakfast, love?'

'I'm fine, thank you.'

Kaleb opened his mouth as though to add his own answer but I reached out to tap at his elbow, and pause him.

'She didn't ask you.'

The dining room no longer looked fit for purpose. What had once been a brilliant white space, colour blocked with varying shades of mustard yellow, was now a light-grey boardroom with a charcoal-coloured feature wall at one end. The family photographs had been stripped – even Ryan's – and instead the walls were bare, cold, bar one single line drawing of a female that was framed and hanging on the wall opposite the window. The table, sans the usual runner and place-settings that Freya once kept there as standard, had been stripped too. In the centre of it there was a large tray with another teapot I didn't recognise, two cups, two saucers; no sugar bowl, which spoke to her familiarity with us both. At the far end of the table was where Freya had clearly nested already; a teacup and saucer sat alongside an open A4 pad, with different coloured pens alongside it. She looked ready to minute the meeting and I wondered whether she was ready to take down anything she might be able to use against him at a later divorce hearing.

'I've been rearranging things,' Freya said as she sat, as though sensing mine and Kaleb's shared appraisal of the space. It wasn't until she was sitting, though, that I noticed there was something else missing from the room too. Where there had once been six chairs around the table – always ready for company – there were now only three, one of which was already occupied by Freya. She sat at the head of the table. Midway down, perfectly centred, there was another chair facing towards the window; then, on the opposing head of the table, there was the third chair. She had literally engineered a face-off – with me in between.

'I'll sit here then, shall I?' I pulled out the middle chair.

'I think that would be best, Annie, please.'

Kaleb quietly took the remaining seat. He already looked ashamed, uncomfortable. *This is nothing,* I thought then. Freya was guns-loaded and ready for him with a stern set expression. She turned to a fresh sheet of paper and then sipped her tea, cleared her throat.

'Kaleb–'

'Freya, I know you don't want to hear this,' he started then, desperate tones pouring out of him. Though I thought as an opener it probably wasn't his best chance of winning her around. 'The... the thing, the fling, it's over with. I know what you saw the other day, and I know how it looked. But it was just... overfamiliarity, it was nothing, nothing that mattered. You...' It was the first time he looked right at her, and although I hated the reaction, I found that I felt something like sympathy for the bloke. 'You're what matters, Frey. Our boy, he's what matters.'

'Mattered.'

Kaleb pulled his eyebrows together. 'Matters. Freya, he *still* matters.'

'Kaleb, while Freya appreciates the affair needs to be discussed, the matter at hand here is how to handle Ryan's memorial service at the school. She'd like for that to be the focus of this, for the time being.' I used my best mediator voice; I'd been given clear instructions before this started. The school had called Freya to invite her and Kaleb to a memorial service they were planning to orchestrate for Ryan; they were both invited, to see the outpouring of love and support felt around their son.

'Despite him giving the entire school the clap,' Freya had added, drunkenly, when she called me to explain two nights before.

'We're going to have to talk about it sometime, Frey.'

'Annie…' was all she said in response.

'Kaleb, are you free to attend the memorial service with Freya?' I asked, again following orders. I was already going; Freya expected it, and I had no reason to refuse. I hadn't yet decided how to get Jessica out of attending though. She must know about it; it would have travelled around the school already by now. But it was also the sort of triggering nightmare she didn't need at the moment – or ever. 'It's happening next week, next Wednesday,' I added.

'Of course I'm free, Freya, I… I wouldn't miss something like that.'

'Do you want to meet me there or meet me here and one of us can drive in?' Freya asked for herself, and she looked poised to take down his answer in note form. I couldn't understand why, unless it was a power move – or a way of not looking at him, lest she turn to stone. 'I wasn't sure whether you'd be driving in from work. The memorial isn't until lunchtime.'

'I can take the day off?' He looked at me before he looked at Freya; I wasn't sure why. 'Then maybe we can talk before, or after, or…'

Freya lifted her head and stopped him. 'I don't think that's a good idea.'

'Frey, come on. We're going to need each other.'

'We're going to need someone, you're right.' She lowered her gaze then, and began to doodle on her notepad; so it *was* all about distraction. 'You have someone, I have someone.'

'She's referring to me before you get any ideas,' I added. I knew she was baiting him. 'Kaleb, I think Freya's main focus here is getting through the next few days, memorial service included. Freya,' I turned to her, 'I think Kaleb's main concern is that the affair goes undiscussed for too long and nothing gets resolved around that issue.'

'So you're on his side now?'

'I'm on no one's side, sweetheart, that's the point of me being here.' Though we all knew that wasn't true. 'Is there a time, after the memorial service, when you think you might be able to talk to Kaleb, about what's happened?' She locked eyes with me and I tried to give her a pleading look. She didn't need to forgive the bastard – her words – but at some point, I thought, she was at least going to have to talk to him.

'I suppose–' She started, but the shrill of the house phone ringing somewhere in the hallway cut through her. 'You'll have to excuse me.'

Kaleb waited until she was out of the room before collapsing onto the table. His head was pressed hard against the wood and his arms thrown out in front of him at odd angles. 'I've fucked it, Annie.' He looked up at me then, his eyes already burnt red from tears that hadn't come yet, but they looked imminent. 'I've fucked it entirely, and now I've lost them both.'

I realised then, where my earlier sympathy had come from – and where it came from again now. I, too, was terrified of losing them both. Theo had already gone; long gone, but with no less sting now than when he'd first died. Now, I was feeling around in the corners of a darkness to find a way to shield my daughter from going anywhere too. I couldn't lose them both. But I feared I was about to. And that's when I realised something else; another ugly, horrible thought: I was going to have to help Kaleb.

Freya came to a stop in the doorway as I was reaching across to grab Kaleb's hand. I snatched my arm back as though I'd been caught doing something indecent. But she fixed us with a glassy stare that seemed to look straight through us both.

'Sweetheart?' I clambered up and crossed to her. 'Freya, are you okay?'

'That was the police,' she said, snapping from her trance. 'They've… I think, she said something about taking someone into custody. Or, I don't know, was it custody?' She seemed to be asking me, but I had nothing, could give nothing; other than the fireball-singe of panic in my gut then, at what might be coming next. 'A girl from the party, apparently, a girl… Someone gave them a name, I think.'

'Who?' Kaleb was up by then too. He didn't crowd us but he edged closer. 'Someone who they think hurt Ryan? They've found who hurt Ryan?'

She shook her head. 'It's nothing definite. She said it's a person of interest, I think, someone they're questioning. I… She said she didn't want us to hear rumours, thought it was best coming from them. She didn't… I don't think she said much else. Something about…' She narrowed her eyes and shook her head as though mentally flicking through an archive of the conversation. 'A tip, she said something about a tip. That it was anonymous, but someone called, and…'

I didn't wait for more. Instead, I only pulled her toward me by the shoulders and held her together in a tight enough embrace to catch any more fractures before they could fall. I squeezed her to me, buried my expression in her loose curls, and thanked God that the phone call must have worked.

CHAPTER THIRTY-TWO

'He didn't even know anyone in Leeds.' Freya paced the room, confused-angry-anxious. More information had filtered through in the last two days. There was nothing especially concrete; no arrest warrant, no holding any one person in custody. But Freya had been told that a young woman had become a person of interest in the case; a young woman who, we soon discovered, had recently undergone treatment for Chlamydia. 'Who the fuck is this *Zoe*?' She made the girl's name sound like an accusation. 'Is *she* from Leeds? Who the hell would go all the way to Leeds to call? Who, Annie? Does Jessica know anyone?'

I hadn't spoken to Jessica still. She must know that there was a person of interest in Ryan's case now, because everyone would. The speed at which teenage girls were able to transmit gossip to each other looked to be the same impressive speed that Chlamydia might move through a series of school cohorts; the rate was alarming. There had been another four cases at Jessica's school alone, and there no longer looked to be a question of where or who it had come from – only how to get rid of it. There had been an advisory email from the head sent late last night, encouraging parents to discuss the matter with their children; a caution I imagined most people were keen to avoid.

'She hasn't said, no,' I answered, then I tried to sip my tea, holding the porcelain tight with two hands that persisted in shaking. I passed it off as tiredness the first time Freya noticed and perhaps it was. The Leeds drive had been a long one, though there hadn't been much traffic at that time of the night through to the morning at least. But it had taken even longer still to find a working payphone – one that wasn't covered by security cameras.

'Annie, you need to get some rest.' Freya landed hard on the sofa next to me. 'Look at you, love, you're shaking still.'

'I'm fine.' I took great care in setting the tea down though. 'I'm more worried about you, Frey. Is there anything… I know there's nothing, but, if I *can* do anything.' I had been especially generous with my time over the last nearly-week. Since seeing her and Kaleb together but not, I'd somehow started to feel like there was more than just Ryan's death to atone for. After all, if he hadn't died – *if Jessica hadn't…* – then Freya never would have discovered Kaleb's affair. Though I went back and forth on whether that was better than the hostile territory their home had become in the aftermath of the discovery. She deserved to know, after all. *And Kaleb is a shit whether Ryan is dead or not…* I squeezed my eyes tight shut as though clearing my vision of something. 'Sorry, I said, early onset headache coming in.'

'Go,' she answered, softly. She pulled me to her, and I took great comfort in that closeness for a second then – before reminding myself that I wasn't deserving of it.

'I've got a work meeting this morning anyway.' I stood and straightened out my trousers, with their professional pleats down the centre. I'd been at Freya's since before dawn, watching her pace and pant and pour her heart out about Zoe, Leeds, Zoe, Ryan, poor Jessica. In truth, my own hostile territory of home was becoming a vice around my neck and I had keenly chosen the option of being with Freya over being ignored by my own daughter. The tension was too much to bear, and I wondered when one of us – *which* one of us – would snap. 'I'll come over later?'

'There's no pressure, honestly. The police said they might come today too.'

In which case, I'll definitely be over later. I leaned forward and kissed the top of her head. 'I'll be over.'

The shock of cold air came as a welcome slap when I left. I hadn't driven, so I took my time in a slow saunter home with a winter bite bringing colour back to my cheeks. I hoped by the time I was pushing through my own front door I might feel livened somehow. Instead, I only felt a swell of nerves pushing their small feet against my stomach; when I looked down, I half-expected the bulge of it. My key was hardly wedged in the lock when the front door was yanked away from me, and there stood Jessica – and those small nervous feet kicked me again. A gust of chill made me tense up and I tried to convince myself that it wasn't in part a knee-jerk reaction to this sudden stand-off too. I stepped aside and made way for her.

'You're late for school?' I tried.

'I had some things to sort out.' Her neutral tone was another cold winter slap. I wasn't sure I'd expected an answer at all. 'You've got a work meeting on the calendar?'

'I… This morning, yes. Jess, sorry, what's happening here?'

She looked down at her feet, knocked one boot against the other to create a sound that echoed on the doorstep. 'I've done a lot of thinking, that's all. I'm sorry, Mum.' She looked up at me and managed to stare at me straight. 'I'm sorry for the lot of it. And,' she paused and forced out a slow breath as though steadying herself, 'and I really do love you.'

Jessica launched herself at me then, arms around my neck like a small chimp clinging to its parent in crisis, and I felt my tension ebb. This was the most verbal contact we'd had in days, let alone physical, and the longer she held on, the more I felt my swell of nerves give way to a swell of tears until I was crying into her scarf. I held my breath, to try to hide the shoulder judder of feelings pouring out. But she must have noticed when she pulled away from me.

'We'll talk more later?' I asked, and even I could hear the desperation in me. She only smiled; a thin-lipped expression that highlighted the recent thinness in her face. *I must make more effort in feeding us both; I will try harder,* I promised myself. 'I love you, too, sweetheart. I really do.'

And with that she was gone, leaving me alone with a mascara-tear medley running from my chin and landing on the concrete of our porch step.

It was mid-afternoon by the time I walked through my front door again. The meeting had been fine – a new client in need of content, there was nothing unusual about it – but it had run on for so long that I decided to stop at Freya's on the way home too. The police hadn't been to see her yet; though she had called to check whether they were still coming, and she was greeted with a noncommittal response. I'd entertained the idea of camping out there, hunkering down until the inevitable knock at the front door came. But I couldn't do that for day in, day out, or however long it would take to see whether I really had managed to disappear my daughter from view – if that was something I was ever going to be certain of. Not for the first time, I entertained the possibility that this threat might follow us both for the rest of our lives, and I wondered whether that idea exhausted Jessica as much as it did me. After an hour with Freya – during which time she managed to use Kaleb's name without a sour expression taking over her, which I took to be a sign of something positive – I made my excuses and went home.

It was early for Jessica to be back. But the hum of music from somewhere upstairs gave her away. I had abandoned reprimanding her for leaving school early; I was glad that she was going at all. So I resisted the urge to march upstairs and ask whether this was a free period or a bunk off. Instead, I clicked the heating to high, shrugged my coat off my shoulders and onto the hallway hook, and marched straight into the kitchen. Whether it was the winter cold or the tiredness, or an unforgiving medley of the two, I felt a chill that penetrated through to my core, and a hot water bottle, tea, ten minutes on the sofa was all I hankered for. I rubbed my hands together while the kettle boiled and paced the small squares of the kitchen, keeping my feet inside the outlines of the grout every time, like I might have done as a child – like Jessica had done, too, once upon a time. An acoustic rendition of 'The Way You Make Me Feel' sang out from overhead and though it made a change from the dark atmospheric soundtracks she'd been listening to for the past weeks, when it clicked over and restarted, a small groan fell from me at the thought of listening to the song again. *Bloody teenagers, ruining the best music* was all I could think as I ferreted around the bottom cupboard for a water bottle to fill.

It wasn't until I was leaving the room with hot comfort in both hands that I spotted a sheet of paper on the kitchen table – on my laptop, to be more exact. A spot where it would be impossible for me not to see it. I crossed over and saw my daughter's unmistakable cursive; she'd practised it for so long when she was younger. I heard the same song click over again from her bedroom and I skimmed the note and–

I'm sorry, Mum. I've tried. I've been trying. But I can't live with this. I shouldn't have to. I love you so much. And please know I'm only doing this to make it all easier and to make it all go away. I love you. Don't help.

–the chorus rang out.

The water bottle and hot tea dropped from my hands

respectively; porcelain cracked across the floor and sent dirty brown spilling up the walls and I ran. Along the hallway, up the stairs, along another hallway to the closed bedroom that I smashed open with the force of someone breaking glass for an extinguisher. There was a fire of panic in my chest and a blazing mess of acoustic sounds that hit me like blowback. And there were two empty wine bottles. And there were tablets. And there was–

'Jess? Jessica! Can you hear me? Jess?'

CHAPTER THIRTY-THREE

There is such a uniformity of colour in hospitals that I wondered, sometimes, whether the scheme was NHS-issued. It was something like olive but faded, as though every wall and floor had been left to sun exposure for too long. And my mind staggered back to the last olive waiting room that I'd dragged my wounded daughter to. I was thinking this when the doctor explained to me the procedure required to empty the contents of someone's stomach and somehow thinking, too, how strange it was to be thinking of anything other than what was being explained to me. But the coloured thoughts stopped the information from going in and– *Is this shock?* I wondered, as he clarified for a second time that there was only so much a stomach pump could do but they felt certain that the majority of the toxins had been emptied. *Toxins,* I managed to parrot back, though it took a second for my laboured brain to realise he meant alcohol, and paracetamol, and naproxen, and– *How many tablets had she taken?* But it seemed a silly question to ask. I couldn't see that any pump would have allowed the exact quantity to be tallied, as though the tube freed them one at a time while a nurse counted them into a metal bowl like a child plucking their favourite Skittles from a packet. He used terms like 'poisoning', 'lasting damage' and 'psychiatric evaluation', and I flung them away like the yellow and green ones I never liked the taste of. I only wanted red and purple left behind; I only wanted to know–

'But is she going to be okay?' My voice finally cracked out of me.

The doctor gave me an NHS-issued smile and reached forward to squeeze my elbow in prescribed comfort. 'She really needs to rest at the moment. We'll be keeping her in overnight for observations, too, and she really will need to be evaluated before we can let her go anyway.' He spoke slowly as though my shock had rendered me childlike, and while I would have normally found the tone patronising, instead I found that I was grateful. I thought of dropping to my knees and clinging to his legs when he turned to walk away, though that seemed like a gesture that may only lead to further evaluations.

'Can I see her?' I shouted after him, and he turned.

'She's asleep at the moment. You're welcome to go in, but she really does need to rest.'

When she's sleeping, you should be sleeping. I remembered all of the parenting advice I'd been given when I came home with her swaddled in pink blankets that I secretly hated, and I nodded my slow understanding to this new doctor now. I sank back into the cradle of the seat outside my daughter's room, held my head in my palms, and waited. A nurse crept in, then crept out again, confirmed she was still sleeping, and all I managed was another nod. The doctors had pumped my words clean out of me.

When I looked up to check how many more minutes had ticked by, my view was obscured by Freya running down the corridor – Kaleb trailed behind wearing the same solemn expression that I could imagine Theo wearing in this situation. I had managed to text her – *Jess. Hospital. Overdose.* – but I didn't know whether she'd come. I soon shook that thought anyway. *Of course she was going to come.*

'Jesus Christ, Ann,' she dropped to her knees in front of me, 'what the fuck happened?' She pulled me to her before I could answer, and my incoherent ramblings fell into her hair. Over her shoulder I could see Kaleb talking to a nurse; he'd decided to go the sensible route for information.

'I told her we're family,' he said when he came to settle down next to me, 'I hope you don't mind.'

'Of course she doesn't mind,' Freya said, 'we are.'

I pushed my hair away from my face and dropped back in my seat. Then I stared at the ceiling and managed, 'She was listening to their song.'

'Love, I'm sorry, I...'

'"The Way You Make Me Feel".'

'Hers and Ryan's song,' Kaleb finished the explanation for me. I felt him lean his weight against me and I dropped my head to his shoulder. 'It wasn't that crap acoustic version, was it?'

'Have you seen her?' Freya interrupted.

'She's sleeping.'

I saw her shoot a look at Kaleb, then back to me. 'Shouldn't someone be in there? For when she wakes up?'

I didn't know whether she was offering. But I couldn't see how waking up to see Freya's worried expression would be a welcome sight for the girl who tried to kill herself from guilt.

'Let me?' She squeezed my knee and stood. *I don't deserve this kindness* was all I could think. The thought thrashed around inside me; it weighed me down when I tried to stand with her. 'Love, honestly,' she eased me back, 'I told you, we're family. I'll call you in as soon as she–' *I don't deserve this kindness.* '–and when she's awake you can come in and talk to her. I won't disturb her. And Kaleb can stay out here with you–' *I don't deserve this kindness.* '–won't you, Kaleb?'

He murmured in agreement but I had no idea what he was agreeing to.

'Freya, I can't let you go in there,' I tried but I could hear the weakness in me. I coughed to clear away the nerves-guilt-*I don't deserve this kindness*. 'Freya, seriously–'

'Annie, seriously–'

'Freya?' The strangled sound came from inside Jessica's room, and the three of us froze stock still like teenagers caught in a horror scene. 'Freya?'

I sank into my seat. *She didn't want me*. She wanted–

'Love, I'll go in and check on her and then I'll be right back to you, and you can go in, okay?'

Not okay, I wanted to say, none of this is fucking okay. But the part of my throat responsible for vibrating protests only constricted, and I felt it tighten every time I opened my mouth. Freya kissed me on the forehead, then squeezed Kaleb's shoulder on her way past him. What a sad thing, I thought then, that this had somehow brought them back to each other – for a moment or two, at least. The hospital door opened a crack somewhere behind me and the hinges complained at the movement.

'I can't let her go in there,' I said weakly to Kaleb, without looking at him. I couldn't stand to look his sympathy in the eye. He said something in answer but I blocked it out with clusters of cotton-wool panic balled into my ears. 'I can't let her…' I was up and out of my seat, but stunned by the sight of the part-open door. I wanted to move forward but I was terrified of what scene waited on the other side; something I imagined was infinitely worse than this safe distance. I felt Kaleb squeeze my hand and tug, as though leading me away, but still I lingered on the threshold.

'Is Mum angry?' I heard then, and I snatched my hand away from Kaleb's and reached for the door but found I could only make it as far as the frame. I leaned heavily against it and listened as my best friend reassured my daughter, cooed over her, said, 'None of us are angry with you, lovely, lovely Jessie.'

And for the first time since finding her those hours ago, I started to cry.

'Freya, I need to tell you…'

'Ann, come on, take a minute.'

Kaleb stood behind me, his hands cupped around the balls of my shoulders. I didn't realise how much I was crying until I heard the friction of my coat rubbing against his palms. *She's going to confess,* I thought then, with another wave of quiet tears, *she's going to confess, and I'm not going to stop her.* It was a hideous ugly thought that rendered me mute; dumbstruck and useless. Everything in me pulled further towards the door but nothing in me moved because the echo of another thought, a worse thought still, somehow, held me back: *She's going to confess, and this might be the only way for me to keep her now.* If Jessica couldn't live with what she'd done, and I couldn't let her die, then how else would we get through this haunted forest of guilt unless that was pumped out of her too? I lowered my head and tried to force free a long breath but it was jagged, catching at my insides.

'Jessie,' Freya cut off whatever Jessica had been saying, 'I need to tell *you* something, love, okay? Are you listening?' I wanted to peer through the crack and watch them, but it felt too much like an intrusion on something I was already unwelcome to. 'Lovely, sweet Jessie. It isn't worth your life.'

Air sputtered out of me and I slapped a hand across my mouth to shield the sound. Kaleb's grip tightened around me, but no matter how hard he tried to move me away I found that I was fixed.

'Freya, you don't understand.'

'No, *you* don't understand. It has *killed* us to lose our Ryan, I know that, and I see that, and I understand, Jessie, okay, I understand.' There was a pause, the muffled sound of crying, but I couldn't work out which one of them it came from. 'But we will get through this because we have to. Not getting through it, Jessie, it just isn't an option. And– Don't interrupt me.' A long pause followed – or at least it felt long on the fringes. 'And he would never, *ever*, want you to go with him. Whatever he did, whatever he'd been up to, and don't you think for a second that I don't know by now what he was up to, but whatever he was up to, he *loved* you, Jessie. You were his ride-or-die, didn't he say that?'

I thought I heard a noise like a laugh but I couldn't be sure past the blood rushing through my ears.

'I loved him so much, Freya. *So* much and I…'

'I know, baby girl, I know.' I braved a look through the door and into the darkened room; dimmed sleeping conditions for the patient. Freya was sitting on the edge of the bed cradling Jessica. 'I know you loved him, and that's exactly why you have to keep living for him, okay? You and I,' she pulled away to get a view of Jess's face and I could see her then, too, 'we're going to make sure everyone remembers him, right? And whatever happens, long-term, whatever happens, he is *always* going to be with us, and in us, and no fucker is going to take that.'

They locked eyes, and I watched as something bubbled to the surface in my daughter. 'I'm so sorry, Freya… for everything… everything I did to him and… I'm just so sorry and… I would never, *ever*, want to hurt to him. I would have never wanted that.' The words were thick with mucus and feeling, and interrupted with harsh breaths as she tried to speak through her tears. 'I'm just sorry.'

Freya pulled her close again. 'I know that, Jessie, and wherever Ryan is, he knows it, too, okay? He knows that all the arguments and tiffs and… whatever else ever happened between you two, he knows.'

My heart pulsed in my throat as I watched my daughter the murderer stare into the face of the woman whose son she'd killed. It was a mother's nightmare, this pregnant heavy wait for a confession to spill. But instead of anything more, Jessica only nodded, slowly, as though a dawn was rising. She dropped back into bed and said, 'Can you get Mum for me, please? I'd really like to...' She petered out as I pushed the door open, and both of us managed to force a tired smile for the other.

It hadn't been the confession I was braced for. But I hoped this might be absolution.

PART 4

AFTER

NO NEW LEADS FOR SLAIN SCHOOLBOY

Police confirmed today that a suspect in the Ryan Tucker murder investigation has now been released.

A young woman from the local area was called in for questioning following an anonymous tip, that named her as a sexual partner of the victim. The police have not been able to confirm or deny the suspect's relationship to the deceased. However, sources close to the case have suggested that the woman may also have information pertaining to the recent spike in Chlamydia cases in the local area, since traced back to the victim's school. When this was posed to the investigating officers, they refused to make a formal statement on the matter.

Ryan's mother, Freya Tucker, commented: "The police are doing everything they can and we appreciate that. Though we know, too, that the longer the investigation lasts the less likely they are to find the culprit at all, and that's a difficult thing to make peace with." Freya Tucker urged anyone with additional information about Ryan's death, or the party that prefaced Ryan's death, to contact the police as a matter of urgency.

At this stage, investigations are ongoing. However, the police are not believed to have any further suspects at this time.

CHAPTER THIRTY-FOUR

I drove home from Bristol thinking about misdirection. While I had been looking in one direction – managing counselling appointments; monitoring food and alcohol intake; listening to late-night confessions – my daughter had grown up in the other. In the six months since Ryan, Jessica had somehow recovered – though it hadn't been a linear journey. There had been the psychiatric evaluations, the follow-up consultations, the side-eye looks from school friends and even their parents, all of whom were judging her, albeit not in the way she wanted. And during a 2am conversation three nights after she'd been released from hospital, she explained that was what it was all about: a need for judgement.

Jessica believed she needed to be punished; I believed she already had been.

'You don't need to hand yourself a life sentence,' I'd promised her.

'You have to say that.'

'No, Jessie, I don't.' I'd tightened my grip on her knee and waited for her stare to settle on me. 'When you're doubting whether you need to be punished or not, remember that I *chose* to help you. Remember that I *chose* to keep you safe. If *you* don't believe you need to be protected over punished, you can at least trust that I do.'

From there it had been a brick-by-brick journey, and with those bricks we'd started to make a road. To my surprise, Freya was instrumental in it all, too, and while Jess found that difficult to begin with, she soon came round to it. It gave Freya something to focus on – while Zoe Gallows was being interviewed, released, and then re-interviewed, following further statements that placed her with Ryan only moments before his death. There were no other suspects; she was the obvious culprit. Though the police had admitted to Freya they didn't have enough to formally charge her, they had told her that Zoe was another Chlamydia case; a young woman without an alibi; a half-arse drug dealer to kids younger than herself – a crime she *was* being charged for, it turned out.

And there's that misdirection again.

I pulled into the cemetery and straight into the space alongside Freya's car. She was already lingering on the pathway to the graves, with an outlandish bunch of flowers in tow. She smiled when she saw me, a nervous gesture, I thought. This was her first time visiting Ryan since he'd been buried. When she asked me to come with her, I'd suggested that she might like to take Kaleb instead – admittedly, my motives were many and varied. They'd been in couples' counselling for three months now and while a shared visit to their son's grave didn't reach the criteria for a date – something they had managed two or three times already – I still thought it might be an important thing for them to share. Though Freya disagreed. Too much, too soon, she said, and then she asked me again whether I'd come.

It was a landmark day for everyone. Three hours before meeting Freya, I had been en route to the University of Bristol where Jessica was now enrolled for three years' study – an unconditional offer, given the circumstances, though that was something else she felt she didn't deserve. She was down there for a taster weekend, but we'd taken the essentials – a toaster and a kettle, and emergency changes of clothing – to leave in what would eventually be her room for the next year. On the journey there she'd been a nervous animal, flinching at every noise, staring from the passenger window like a wounded dog travelling to a veterinary clinic for what it knew would be the final time. But when we entered the car park for her allocated building, we'd been greeted by friendly smiles, waves from people she didn't yet know, and a young woman who soon introduced herself as Babs, the student ambassador for Jessica's housing block. Jess pushed her hair behind her ears, looked at the ground, and introduced herself.

'There's no need to be nervous,' Babs said, the smile still fixed in place, 'we're a friendly bunch in B block. We all take care of each other here.'

I smiled, too, and tried to push down the prison connotations of B block that chased around my head. 'I'm Annie.' I held out a hand to her, which she reciprocated with confidence. I had visions, then, of Jessica coming home from the weekend a changed woman, smiling wide with loud excitement. But I cautioned myself and borrowed from Freya's thinking: too much, too soon.

'She'll settle in fine.' Freya pulled me into a hug as soon as I arrived next to her. 'She's doing better, Annie, I know it, you know it. She'll get her confidence back now she's there. She'll be drinking and...' She petered out when she realised the error in her optimism. 'Well, she won't be drinking. But you know what I mean,' she unleashed me from the hug then, and smoothed down my hair either side of my face, 'she'll be mingling, making friends.'

'I know, I know,' I answered, my tone petulant. Though I hoped to God she was right.

Freya looped an arm through mine and angled me towards

the pathway. The pretzel packet crinkled in my pocket when she pushed against me. 'We've all got to start moving on, haven't we?'

The question was rhetorical, I thought, but I murmured in agreement all the same. I let her guide me through the graveyard to where Ryan was rested. Neither of us managed small talk along the way; the silence of us spoke more. I felt her tense when the unsettled grave came into view.

'It's not right, Ann,' she managed then. 'It's just not right.'

'I know, sweetheart.' As though having issued each other with a silent cue we came to a stop then, twenty paces or so from Ryan. I couldn't go any further, and I prayed she wouldn't expect me to. 'You can do this.' I turned and set a hand either side of her face to hold her gaze steady with my own. 'Go, see your boy. I'll go, see my man. Then we're going to go home and get good and drunk, okay?' We both managed a laugh, though mine burnt up my throat like a bad wine that left me breathless. I forced a steady exhale. 'Go, I'll be ten rows away.'

I watched her tread closer to the gravesite, waited until the flowers were being lowered, then I scarpered like an interrupted squirrel. I hadn't brought a blanket with me – I didn't know how long we'd be staying – but still I lowered myself to the damp ground when I got to Theo's headstone. By this time of year the earth had normally dried out, but a wet early summer meant that I could still feel mud and grit soaking through the denim of my jeans. It had been two months since I'd last visited, and the headstone looked worse for wear. There was a growing to-do list on the kitchen table at home – finish the content for the Tengo contract; replace lightbulb in bathroom; check in with Kaleb – and I mentally added *call the stonemason for T.* That came above Kaleb; most things did, and had done for weeks. But my attitude to forgiveness had changed in the last eight months or so.

Kaleb had, in a drunken stupor, reminded me one evening that I was his friend as well. Jessica had been sound asleep when the doorbell rang out, and I rushed to it, expecting a distraught Freya on the other side. I'd become accustomed to one or both of them being in a state of some distress; though even Freya usually called before turning up late into the night. But there, instead of my best friend, I'd found her cheating husband. Kaleb had been dishevelled, leaning hard against the doorframe to hold his weight up.

'You shouldn't be here,' I'd said, my tone flat. I didn't know what his logic was, but I was already irritated with him for thinking I could be of any use to him. Instead of heeding what I'd said as a warning, though, he pushed his way through into the hall, muttering something about having nowhere else, no one else, as he went.

'You need to help me get her back, Annie.' Kaleb had landed so hard in one of my kitchen chairs that I'd worried the legs might give out. 'You *need* to help me.'

'I need to give you coffee and send you on your way.' I was faced away from him, filling the kettle already.

'You owe me,' he'd said, then, and I'd frozen.

'I'm sorry?' I managed to look him, and with the black bead eyes that you only ever find in a drunk person, he stared back.

'You owe me,' he said again, leaving a deliberate pause between each word. 'I cannot lose my *wife* when I have lost my *son*.'

'I'm missing the part when I owe you shit, Kaleb.'

He laughed then, a huff of a noise, ran his hands over his face and dropped his head back, to stare at the ceiling rather than me. 'I have lost my son because of your *daughter*.'

And just like that, the worst thing imaginable had finally happened: someone knew.

I hadn't managed to say much after that. Kaleb, seeing my stunned expression, I suppose, pushed back from the table and managed to stagger over to me. I jerked my head back, placing distance between myself and his beer breath as he explained:

'Losing one of them is one thing, but I cannot lose them both. And *I* know that *you* know exactly what I mean.'

Of course I did. After two coffees he explained to me how obvious it had been, to him, that Jessica wasn't only grieving: she was guilty of something. Leave it to the liars to recognise their own. It wasn't until the new girl – Zoe – had turned up out of nowhere that he wondered whether Jessica might actually have had something to do with what happened though. 'Something about it didn't sit right, Ann, no matter what the police said.' Then when Jessica had tried to – tried to leave, 'That's when I knew. You don't go killing yourself over grief, not when you're a smart kid like her.' *Not so smart not to have killed someone,* I'd thought as I'd filled the kettle for the second time. Kaleb didn't want much in exchange for his silence; only for me to softly nudge Freya towards forgiving him, gifting him another chance.

'You know as well as I do, no one can make Freya do anything she doesn't want to.'

'I'm not asking you to *make* her do anything, Annie.' Somehow, the brittle edges of our conversation had softened enough by then for Kaleb to reach across my kitchen table and grab my hand. 'I'm just asking you to try.'

'Give the man his favour, Annie,' Theo might have said, then, 'Keep her safe.'

Once settled in front of his grave, I ferreted around in my front pocket and pulled free a packet of chocolate-covered pretzels. It was a variation on his old classic. *But things change,* I thought as I tugged the bag open. I placed a single pretzel on the ground in front of his headstone and managed a smile. 'Right, where to start...'

THE END

ALSO BY CHARLOTTE BARNES

Suspense Thrillers:

Intention

All I See Is You

Sincerely, Yours

The Things I Didn't Do

Safe Word

Penance

Crime:

The DI Melanie Watton Series

The Copycat (book one)

The Watcher (book two)

The Cutter (book three)

A NOTE FROM THE PUBLISHER

Thank you for reading this book. If you enjoyed it please do consider leaving a review on Amazon to help others find it too.

We hate typos. All of our books have been rigorously edited and proofread, but sometimes mistakes do slip through. If you have spotted a typo, please do let us know and we can get it amended within hours.

info@bloodhoundbooks.com

Printed in Great Britain
by Amazon

26297383R00138